GREASEPAINT

HANNAH LEVENE

GREASEPAINT

NIGHTBOAT BOOKS
NEW YORK

ISBN: 978-1-64362-213-2

Cover photograph: "Della and Scooter" by Del LaGrace Volcano.
June 1981. Collection of the Lesbian Herstory Archives.
Courtesy of the artist.

Design and typesetting by Kit Schluter
Typeset in Adobe Caslon Pro

Cataloging-in-publication data is available
from the Library of Congress

Nightboat Books
New York
www.nightboat.com

"Frankie's name isn't Frankie, of course. I never knew a Frankie, though I know that there were some in the clubs. And our conversations are collages of many chats over the years."

LISA E. DAVIS

from "The Butch as Drag Artiste:
Greenwich Village in the Roaring Forties"

FEATURING

THE ANARCHISTS

FRANKIE GOLD, the singer
SAMMY SILVER, the piano player
SID STEIN, the doer
ROZ, the butch belle juive

THE ALL-AMERICANS

MARG, the All-American
TEDDY, the All-American
LAUR, the All-American
VIC, the All-American

THE BOP

LOUIS BROOKS, the bartender
HARRY HARLEM, the piano player
SAMMY, the piano player

AND

LILY, the anarchist

THE PLAYERS

[Meeting of the BOP at Louis' Place: A Songbook]
Oh baby it's another night at Louis' place and look
who's meeting in the corner by the jukebox it's the
Butch Piano Player's Union, it's the BOP! It's Louis
herself and Sammy her best piano player and some
empty chairs and who's coming now? It's Sammy
Silver! What's that in her hands? Oh baby it's a pile
of papers hot off the press. Sammy holds the papers
in her arms piled up under her chin and she uses
her chin to hold them as they wobble about and
she wiggles under them it's the IWW the Butch
On Piano faction it's all the piano players in town
who wear their hair short and their shirts pressed
and who the ladies love it's the BOP. "Enough song
sheets to fill a concert hall" plunk, puts the pile in
the center of the little round table in the corner by
the jukebox. Now Louis is calling the meeting to
order. Louis: "I said shake rattle and roll" everybody
else: "I said shake rattle and roll" Louis: "It's the

dance sensation" everybody else: "That's sweeping the nation" "And talking of nation—" "Imagination?" "No!" "Assassination?" "No!" "Consternation?" "NO!" "Indoctrination?" "Discrimination?" "Domination?" "No no no. Understand! The formation of peoples into nations is an objective law of social development. A nation is an historically constituted stable community of people based on THREE main characteristics: [SHAKE] a common territory [RATTLE] a common language [ROLL] a common character manifested in common features in a national culture. Since the development of imperialism, the liberation of the oppressed nations has become a question whose final resolution would only come through proletarian revolution. Get out in that kitchen and rattle those pots and pans" everybody else: "Get out in that kitchen and rattle those pots and pans." What's cookin comrades? Oh here's a late comer, it's Harry, the butchest piano player in town always strolling in late and asking what's cookin comrades. Harry made the girls melt like tears into a pillow. This week in the newsletter Sammy'd interviewed Harry about the current touring production of Porgy and Bess whose final staging would be in Leningrad. "I think we should talk" Sammy said "me being a Jew I mean sort of and you being a Black butch in America about Summertime" "You don't think we should talk about Sportin Life? Us being queers?"

"Queers being what we have in common I thought maybe we could talk about our differences instead, me being an anarchist—I mean totally—and you being well, a different sort of revolutionary" "War sure is cold" "Sure is. When we play a song like Summertime are we as Jewish and Black Americans collaborating? and can we ever collaborate when Jews can be white in America when to be white in America is to be safe and to have opportunity which is the opposite of what it means to be Black in America, I mean *constitutionally* you understand, I mean *as it is written you understand.*" This would be edited out of the final interview to be printed in the newsletter of the BOP, distributed to its twenty to twenty-five fluctuating members with updates on which bars were allowing access to a piano for practice and when, a song sheet of the latest hit, who was looking for a partner to compose with, calls for auditions, a tear away for annual membership fees to be posted, and any other business. It would be printed: Sammy Silver: When we play a song like Summertime, are we, as Jewish and Black Americans, collaborating? There in the moment when they're talking, Harry would reply after sitting and thinking, chewing at her lip a little and stroking her chin. Harry was square, her shoulders were a long line and she wore a suit jacket and suit trousers in dark blue with her Communist Party membership details typed on silk and sewn into the lining. Harry came from a long line of Harrys but no one knew where Harry came from. Harry's shoulders were a long line. When Harry licked her lips the girls melted "You think Gershwin and you think assimilation" "There are rumors he's a Bolshevik" "I never heard them and don't you think I would have?" "Everybody's listening" "Sure. But you hear Gershwin you hear rhapsody in blue, an American symphony" Harry said "Gershwin thought that because he was an American he could use Black bodies like a real American man" "There are rumors he's a homosexual" "There's plenty of American homosexuals" "They call it unamerican" "They call it lots of things, in fact you name it I've been called it" "So you're saying it isn't a collaboration" "You ever use Sophie Soap?" "Sure" "You know that soap on the soap box? Ok she's a pink block of soap and o-*kay* she's got suds in all the right places, but the way she's holding her own little Sophie Soap in her Sophie hand like it's a mitt? I mean that Sophie Soap is a dyke no doubt about it. But heterosexuals use Sophie don't they?" "Sure" "So I can play Summertime if I like" "You're saying you can use Gershwin the way Gershwin used you?" "I'm saying what was Gershwin's isn't Gershwin's anymore, you can mimeograph off the whole score, his whole American rhapsody and paste your house with it, is it collaboration then? No it's repurposing. It's the redistribution of wealth that's what it is" "But what do you think it sounds like Harry? Like jazz or like, like my uncle Herschel?" "A whole lot of music in America sounds like your uncle Herschel Sam. Gershwin shouldn't say he's making American music. He shouldn't sell his music like that. America doesn't deserve it." "America doesn't deserve you either Harry, you play piano like it's playing itself." That's how the interview would end, printed in the newsletter, followed by a couple of lines on each of the union members involved saying something like *this interview was conducted by Sammy Silver* (stage name) *and Harry Harlem* (stage name). *Harry Harlem is a founding member of the BOP. Harry plays piano solo and composes. Harry was for a time the secretary of the BOP, now replaced by our current secretary Louis Brooks. Sammy Silver is the newest member of the BOP, she plays piano in a duo and is responsible for the printing of our monthly newsletter.*

Of course there was the stage which allowed you to act how you liked and to dress how you liked in costumes which Frankie did, though she looked like Frankie whatever she was wearing. "I've seen you." "Yeah?" "Yeah I've seen you." "Where?" "I've seen you do [blank]" "Yeah I've done [bang bang bang went the trolley]" "Yeah I've seen you do [ding ding ding went the bell]" "Yeah that was me" "Hey you were good!"

"I was good?" "You were good!" "Oh I'm good?" "Yes you are!" "Who me?" Frankie pointed a thumb into her chest at the bar after her show with a free bottle of beer and her face freshly washed. She'd been [blank] tonight. Everybody'd clapped and laughed with her and Sammy Silver [give it up for Sammy over here] and they gave it. "Whaddyu think about give, Joanne?" "About give?" "Yes. About *give*" "You mean *giving* Frankie Gold?" "No not *giving* not necessarily, I mean give like how your pants give or your pajamas" "My pajamas?" "Yes how they give whaddyu think" Frankie said "about that?" "I think it's kind of them to let me in, don't you think it is?" "Yes! Yes I do Joanne I think give is terribly kind." Frankie is a soft butch in soft shirts and soft leather shoes. Frankie'd been an anarchist before she'd been a butch and now she was both she couldn't see the difference anymore. Frankie had been born an anarchist like people are born Catholic. She'd learnt the word OPPRESSION the way other children learn mnemonics for planets— One Person Picks Roses Each Sunny Sunday In Omaha Nebraska One Person Picks Roses Each Sunny Sunday In Omaha Nebraska—so when it came to meet her she recognized it, bending to pick roses in the sun. Hey I saw you! Who me? Yeah up there! Up there? Yeah! You're the singer shake hands clap backs. Interrupting what she was about to say which was where the boys are my true love

6

will be he's striding down some street up town and I know he's waiting there for me she did that one, the hits and standards and stage show skits. She did Annie Get Your Gun tonight. Asking the audience "Are there any Annie Oakleys out there this evening who'd like to come up on stage?" picking a girl (One Person Picks Roses Each Sunny Sunday In Omaha Nebraska) and they sang *anything you can do I can do better I can do anything better than you* Annie from the audience: *no you can't* Frankie: *yes I can / no you can't / yes I can* and the crowd thought it was a riot. It was a song which spoke to the heart of its audience, those prone to strutting to prove they could walk. Frankie had felt ecstatic when she'd heard that song. She knew that if they put it in their act that it'd be a hit because the butches would know that it was about them. Frankie had been able to see the stage lighting and the set and the way it was dressed before she'd ever stepped into it. To her it was obvious, she wore cowboy and top hats and other American props and the crowd laughed, sometimes some of them cried. But Frankie wanted them to see what she could see, how easily it could topple down if they only realized it was theirs to reach out and touch. Can't you see it? No you can't, yes I can! No you can't, yes I can! The crowd loved it, they howled. They did the high bit—*any note you can sing I can sing higher*—and got higher and higher and Frankie hit all the notes and

7

they did the softer bit and Frankie sang softer and softer and the bar went quiet and Sammy pressed the keys on the piano so gently they slipped barely out of time, a delay between touching the keys and the hammer hitting the strings. And when they did the bit about clothes Frankie sang it alone, really meaning it, feeling it suddenly more acutely in the place where her heart actually was—*Anything you can wear I can wear better*—Frankie touching the lapels of her jacket—*in what you wear I'd look better than you*—just to touch the knot in a tie which she did or tip a hat to put your hands in your pockets it took your breath away to do that to put your hands in your pockets. Applause! Applause! And somebody standing ready by the jukebox who knew it was time to start it playing again and Frankie touching Sammy on the shoulder on the way off the stage to go back to a little bathroom the staff got to use, to wash her face off, slick her hair back, to change her clothes. And the lights on the stage going down and in the bar going up: "I think give is relaxing" Frankie said "don't you Sammy?" "Sure" "I think if we're going to change the world we have to pay attention to the way the world is made." No one in the bars wanted this type of chat, most people didn't want to talk at all but Frankie kept talking anyway Sammy was listening she'd heard it all before of course but she was and Joanne'd get a kick out of it maybe while polishing glasses. "*I've got the sun in morning and the moon at night*, it's such an American thing to sing, you aren't lucky because you've got the sun! Fuck! Everybody has the sun sometimes!" Thinking lucky was to do with sunshine was what kept people thinking there was no need, no need to talk about it, no need to think about it! Everybody in the goddam bar had nothing but this! And there was no way the sun could get into this basement or any of the other bars all in the basements, all with one way·in and no way out you know, you've heard, you know about that about how there was a way in and that was hopeful but it was the same way as the way out and sometimes you couldn't. You didn't. "The world's made of plates right?" "Made of plates?" "Tectonic plates and what do they do?" "You gonna tell me?" "They move about don't they?" "Do they?" "Yes they move, they shift about because things change Joanne, things change and we can't stay rigid through that pretending they don't, haven't you had a bad back before?" "Before? How about now?" "Exactly it's because you didn't bend properly isn't it? Because you stayed too rigid bringing the boxes of beer in, because the world put too much pressure on you, that's why you're hurt, because you got tired and stiff and it's all changing all the time isn't it Jo? You can't just stand still and take it you've got to, we all have to think more about *give*." Frankie talked and talked and Joanne felt the touch of somebody recognizing she was hurt. It's not insightful, Frankie would have said if Joanne had said it aloud, everybody's hurt. It's not the exception, Joanne, it's the rule, pain's the rule and we're all under it. The next night in a different bar they do it again. Frankie walks onto the stage to Sammy playing there's no business like show business like no business I know and she takes the mic singing lets goo oonn withh the shhoowww. *There's no people like show people they smile when they are low*, she sang and smiled. "We aren't show people Sam, we're no people." She thought that people must look at them like Jews and she hated that, a couple of Jews named Silver and Gold. Sammy's surname wasn't Silver of course, but it could have been. Frankie thought that if she was up on stage and someone came into the bar looking to punch a queer or failing that a communist or failing that a Jew she'd be a real prize, a jackpot, three fruits all in a line. Someone like Laur would worry that thoughts like that might somehow summon a violence they were all trying their hardest to avoid. Laur having still a faint feeling of the lord and of the devil but Frankie didn't have an ounce of that. Any room could change into any room. Really it was the barstool that stayed the same and everything else which changed around it. And Frankie sat on a barstool and let the other parts move, a curtain drawn to let the light in so now she's at the deli and it's morning and the jukebox is still over there, Frankie waved to it, it waved back. And the bar stayed too, only what was behind the bar changed, somebody came on and rolled the booze away and replaced it with jars of pickles. And replaced it with jars of pickles. Frankie thought if she ever left this scene they'd simply pick her up and put a jar of pickles in her place. And the pickle jar sings *anything you can do I can do better, I can do anything better than you.*

[Friday Night: Butch Night Out] Dinner at Marg's before hitting the bars. "If I could pass mustard Laur, I'd be a millionaire" Marg jokes and laughs with her hand on her belly. "Thanks Marg, hey you sure are a wise cracker" says Laur. "Yeah Marg" says Vic "No one's heard that one before." Vic looks like a motorbike. She's so butch the steak is hard to swallow (this phrasing is common in butch crowds: so and so's so butch she showers in a raincoat, so and so's so butch she won't even flip her records, so and so's so butch she . . .) "This steak is swell and the potatoes too, I can't get enough of the potatoes" Laur is the type of boy you bring home to your parents. Teddy agrees "Yeah Marg this is really something. Just how I like it. Do you get fed this well every night, is Suzy really that good?" "She's the best" says Marg. Whole table in unison: "Don't we know it." They go quiet.

[Humming starts up, low and constant and continues through the whole dinner: *you say potato and I say potahto you say tomato and I say tomahto*] Teddy speaks finally "Heard about Louise? She went home to her mother's" "Oh she went home but she'll be back" "Well I hope she doesn't find hellfire at home with her mother" Laur says. "Her mother's not so bad since her father died and her brother married off, hell I think she might be a little bit of bull herself the way we get along" "My mother was definitely a bulldyke, she just never got to know it" Teddy says. "How do you make that out?" "She was as big as me!" They all laugh, even Vic. Teddy is big and soft, he has on a brown suit instead of a leather jacket. He's older than the rest of them, more Marg's age and they're friends mostly because they've been around the bars so long. Teddy likes the younger guys more, they're less depressed than he is and they seem so, so he can't put his finger on it. Teddy's too tired to think too much about it but it's something like going to a good movie and going to a bad one, no no like going to an old movie or going to a new one, the new movie reminds you you're not dead. Teddy spikes his steak on his fork and takes a bite. "Sure is tender" he says. Whole table in unison: "Sure is." [*potato/potahto/ tomato/tomahto*] Laur's here for the food first and the company second because Laur is hungry. You can see Laur's ribs but she'll never take her top off for you. Laur's fine at conversation, needs a meal every Friday, fills in silences, asks questions, makes jokes, lets the gravy from the steak stay in her mouth a little longer and licks mustard off her knife real slow. Laur's body, and she's never been able to say this out loud, never tried, just once or twice so drunk she couldn't speak so it came out slurred which is really how to say it most clearly: Laur's body has always felt like a slur. Like it started at one point but spread out and reached over to another. At best it is misunderstood but mostly it is incomprehensible. It made her feel as if she hadn't spoken at all but she had, she had spoken she had slurred and slurring is a part of speech isn't it? Didn't it come outta my mouth? she thought to herself, storming about in her mind, stomping down its hallways and slamming its doors being angry and butch in her head and it showed. She was a toaster butch, she was butter-side-up butch, how do you like your eggs in the morning butch, meet me by the kitchen sink better than your man but like your man butch, your sweetheart, your heartbreaker, your baby. Laur was worried that sometimes she didn't feel anything at all. Taste was a sense she clung to. She prayed: if I must be numb all over, please god, leave me my tongue. "You're quiet over there Vic" Marg says "what's eating you?" Vic keeps chewing. "How's the bike Vic?" asks Laur "She's a beauty" Vic's heart races at Laur's attention, she swallows down "Did some work on her this weekend, don't get to take her out much in all this rain." Vic has a sharp jaw and a pristine leather jacket, her hair is slicked back and her t shirt is white and all the butches whose t shirts are all white and even Teddy in his white shirt and black tie for all occasions have tucked paper napkins into their collars to eat. "You need a lady to ride with, that'll warm you up" says Marg. It wouldn't seem out of place if Marg started beating her chest like a gorilla, she is upright, shoulders bulky and back. Vic just eats. "What you not interested in girls anymore Vicky?" Marg says. They lock eyes. "She just knows all the good ones are taken. Right Marg?" says Laur. "Keep your mind off my Suzy slick—" "—Who me?" Laur holds her hands up, backs her chair away from the table. "She's a catch isn't she Marg? We meant nothing by it" "What else could we have meant, Margy?" Vic says. Marg stands up. "Pass me back those potatoes will you Vic?" Teddy says. No one moves. "You think you're the biggest bull around here or something?" says Marg "What's big without brains?" Vic says. Marg stands up but more. "Cool it kids" Teddy says "we haven't even hit the bars yet." "Yeah slick. Gotta hit the bars first." No one moves. "Sure we do" Marg says, she takes the pack of cigarettes from the inside pocket of her jacket, sits back down at the table and smokes. "Hey Laur, pass me a beer." "Sure thing boss. Who's for another beer?" Whole table in unison: "Sure thing." Steam traps below the cloud of cigarette smoke and settles above them and Marg's Suzy serves seconds of [*you say potato. I say potahto*] Vic looking across the table, through the steam at Laur [*potato/potahto*] Laur passing Vic the salt [*tomato/tomahto*] Vic using her knife [*potato/potahto*] Vic licking her fork clean [*tomato/tomahto*] Suzy serving thirds of [

The bar's a horse and Frankie wipes it with a rag in the same spot round and round and the bar's delighted and shakes its mane for her. Frankie was the closest thing they had to staff that night when Joanne didn't show up. Please, the owner had pleaded, please Frankie you know where everything is don't you? I'll pay you performer's price not tender price I promise please Frankie I gotta go I gotta be somewhere I can't close the bar, you know the ropes don't you? Frankie'd agreed. "Ganuf" Frankie spoke to the bar-prop "was treated like dirt by everybody, the people who used him to drag their cart about, the kids who saw him tied up and vulnerable, the rider, whoever" Frankie rubs the bar with a rag and the bar nuzzles her hand which is full of peanuts and its big wet lips are gentle. "Everyone treated like shit thinks they're being treated like an animal, exterminated like rats, worked like dogs, caged like lions wouldn't it be better if we just admitted that what we were actually being treated like was men! That man has been treated like shit by man for millennia and still is and will be if we keep imagining that it's only animals that man despises and not the poor or the queers or anybody else who can't prove he's a man as if being a *man* is what'll save you from all the other men well (Frankie might've paused to spit then) being a man won't save you from anything, certainly not from being a horse. You know what I mean?" "Um" the barprop says. Frankie wanted to hear opinions, she was desperate to be challenged, to hear notes that didn't go together, melodies that clashed something, anything. "If" says the person at the bar "if there were a horse in New York" she says "I'd line up like all the other kids who grew up in a city and wait my turn riding him about" "Yes!" Frankie says, she loved that answer! She patted the bar heavily and it shook its behind and whinnied pat pat pat firm nearly setting off into a canter "Yes! You would! And I would too! Of course! because we, you and I, comrade we are the little boy in the book who doesn't beat the horse but steals sugar from his mother's cupboard to feed the horse whilst it's made to wait still harnessed after a long day's work in the street and who the horse shakes its mane for and makes sweet horse sounds" Frankie was excited by the idea of a horse in the city and of young people lining up to pay their respects to it and of the mutual exchange that could happen between a large animal (who reminded her of Roz) and that line of people each one of them getting something different from the horse, some sort of love or kindness or thrill and the horse getting to meet all those people who loved it. At the bar now she imagined the horse as the bartender. The horse on its hind legs with a rag under its hoof making clean circles in the grease, the horse free pouring whisky into a heavy bottomed tumbler and clipping it across the bar into somebody's hand. The horse laying out a square napkin and placing a bottle of beer on it, and clacking coins into the till. Frankie made a crack about giving tips to a horse and the barprop drank up and went. The bar was empty. No one to talk to. The piano was set up and soon Sammy'd come in and play a little. Finished from her day job working as a typesetter at the anarchist newspaper, still with the old gang. Not Frankie though, who never saw any of them and nobody talked about Frankie with Sammy and Sammy and Frankie didn't talk about anybody. Sammy had been a typesetter for the anarchist papers since she was a kid and she'd never left. "Did you know they call it that?" Sammy'd say to girls when they asked her about her work "that stuff between all the letters you can't see? That's called furniture, I always liked that about the job" she'd say dreamily. Sammy was a dreamy type of guy, like a low note on a piano. All she did was keys, keys to type with keys to play piano. She had recurring nightmares about losing her fingers: someone accusing her of something and a judge ruling she'd have each of her fingers chopped off at the guillotine up on the stage in the bar, or worse still she was on stage with Frankie it was the finale a big number and she'd press a key and the finger would *spuk* pop right out of her hand and Frankie'd be singing alone. I need to diversify she'd wake up thinking, shaking her head, clammy, sweat on her forehead the big flop of her hair stuck to her skin, tangled in her eyebrows. "Delores" shaking Delores awake "Delores, Dclores, how many fingers am I holding up?" holding her hands out to show Delores and Delores rolling over, grumbling "Fuck off Sam" grumble. Yeah here she is "Hey Sammy" "Hey Frankie" "Turn the sign round will ya?" [closed] and the lights go down over the bar on Frankie Gold cleaning glasses and up on the stage showing Sammy Silver practicing after hours.

A FRIDAY NIGHT

"Sometimes I think I'm an alien" "How come?"
They're sitting on the steps out the back door of the
bar. Squashed together thigh to thigh in the space of
the door frame, smoking cigarettes. Laur turns to
her, says how come and Vic thinks, clears her throat
to make sure it comes out deep when she says "Because
I sure as hell ain't a woman or a man." Laur swallows.
"Yeah" she says, not like she'd never thought of it,
that maybe she was dead and this was hell, though
sometimes it felt like heaven. And how it felt like
someone had left the iron pressed on her jeans at the
place where Vic's thigh pushed against hers. Vic
smoked. She was the iron definitely. Fuck she'd done
nothing feminine since she could do nothing and still
her head was as domestic as a lapdog, her frame of
reference as closed off as her shitty apartment with
its kitchen by the door and the view of the refrigerator
from the bed. Never thought of being anyone's wife
and still all she could ask was who was the sink? the

vacuum? Laur guffawed and nudged her buddy in the ribs said: "Hell, hear about Josie and her alien shtick?" "Josie who?" "You know Josie, Nel's Josie? Nel told me she likes to do this fantasy bit where Nel's the doctor probing her on an alien spaceship, Nel says she gets a kick out of it too, but hey maybe you should try and muscle in with Josie you might find something out about yourself" Vic smiled a little and shook her head. "When I'm with a girl I don't feel like an alien." She turned to her. "It's all different when there's someone else there balancing you out." Vic and Laur had been hanging around together. They'd see each other on a Friday night then break away from the group, not talking about it just ending up that way. Laur was tired of getting into fights and Vic didn't want to punch anybody anymore. And when it was just the two of them Vic spoke up and Laur liked it. She was always trying to get her to join in with the others, was starting to wonder why she turned up on Fridays at all. But they'd been in touch more and more, just the two of them. Laur could start up a chat with anybody about whatever but she'd never had anyone tell her they thought they were from outer space, she'd never had anyone tell her that before. "I feel balanced now Vic" she said. "Oh yeah?" Vic swallowed. Laur was more earnest than her. She wasn't butch to hide anything just butch because she couldn't hide it. "Yeah, you make sense" "None of this makes any sense, honey." She let it slip out of her mouth without thinking, golden and stretched out. Laur looked over at her and set her back teeth so her jaw looked more like a man's and ran her hand over her chin, "Not anymore" she said. Vic lived alone because she had a job and could afford it. Vic had a job because her father owned a pharmacy and Vic worked in the back dishing out prescriptions and labelling shelves with diacon and pharmacon and vicadil and at work she wore a pharmacist's coat. Mostly she was in the back room, serving customers through a cutout in the wall. People came in, rang the bell and she came to the counter, took their prescription, and got them their drugs. Vic worked for her father and he paid her. Vic was embarrassed to have a father and to have a job. No one else seemed to have a father, maybe some had a mother or a sister and to have a job, sure some had jobs but as secure as Vic's? No way. No everybody else at the bar seemed to have just appeared. Been poured like sand into hourglasses and tipped over. Vic's single father and dead mother and her father's business felt like embarrassingly good fortune, too much to tell anybody about. Anyway she lived alone and she brought girls home. She'd lived with a woman once but she'd got sick of pretending she liked the way she smelt. Vic could cook and clean and she smoked by the window. It had rained after the bar and she'd walked home in it. She smelt like wet leather now by the door pulling off her boots and hanging up her jacket and the drips from her hair and the tip of her nose fell on her white t shirt and made grey holes and Vic thought about her chest and how absurd it felt to have. She opened the fridge and for a second it felt like looking in a mirror. She took out the last of the chicken. It'd dried out on the plate and stuck in her throat. She thought about swallowing and it turned her on, wished she'd picked someone up after all and had someone with her now. She thought about Laur, how her dad would like her, how Laur liked baseball. She called Ruby. "Ruby it's Vic" "So?" "Oh come on what you doin anyway?" "Washing my hair" "No use talking to me like I'm your boyfriend sweety" "No use talking to you at all—" "Don't hang up, come on over Ruby, I'll—" "What?" "I'll make you dinner" "Isn't it nearer breakfast?" "Then I'll make you breakfast" "I'll make my own pancakes, slick" "Not like mine you won't" "Oh yeah what's the secret ingredient, butch?" "Don't like the way butch tastes anymore Ruby slippers?" "What gasoline and hamburger? No slick, I don't" "Well I like to think I'm more tenderloin than hamburger, maybe you could get a taste for that" "Ask me about tenderness another time loverboy. I gotta go." The line went dead and Vic rolled her eyes. She left the phone hanging off the hook and it hummed out into the empty kitchen. She smoked by the window. Laur'd always been dog happy. You know, not quite free but getting a kick out of meeting people like her, dogs too. She liked to growl sometimes, take a bite out of the odd ear chase tails, yeah she did that. Still sat on the step she kept smoking, her hand covering her mouth holding the cigarette between her ring and middle fingers puffing like a little train or let's keep it going, like a little pup smoking a cigarette, a cute cartoon pup with a leather jacket on with all its stuff in its pockets that maybe some advertising guy drew up to sell cigarettes. All sorts of stuff went on in the bar behind her but she kept sitting there. Must have been an hour or so since Vic had gone. How do you explain the elation of a dog seeing another dog? You're walking in the park. So far you've seen only pavements and people's shoes and every now and again something else you wanna sniff. Then suddenly there's this scent in the air then paws, paws on the pavement and you've got paws too, and you wanna cry out I'M A DOG TOO I'M A DOG TOO but all you can do is bark. BARK you say, BARK BARK and your tail starts to wag like a windmill, your heart's racing what's the news? What've you got for me? What can we do together, now, here, on the pavement how can I tell you what it means to me that we're both dogs and we're here together? As it was, Laur had been going to the bars for years now, was a regular face, a little detached but everyone was. No one was there

100 percent she knew that. Everyone would rather have been in a regular bar with the regular people, no one liked the queers, least of all the queers. But that didn't mean they didn't like the gay life, Laur and all her buddies they liked the gay life, getting dressed up to go out and how they teased each other and even being broke, some of them liked that part of it too because when you got rich you couldn't fight anymore, couldn't skip off without anyone noticing you'd gone. Laur figured if you were rich you wouldn't want to. Laur was hungry and rich people weren't hungry like that. She stubbed her cigarette out on the step. "See you next time Jo, I'm done for tonight" "Ok Laurie be careful out there" "You betcha." Down the street to the deli. (Closing time was 4 a.m., when everybody went around to Reuben's, the people who invented the sandwich). The light was different there, pastrami pink, silk pink "Hey Pearl" "Hey Laur, hungry?" "Starved." Frankie was at Reuben's with everybody else. The Reuben really is a fine sandwich. It is associated with kosher-style delicatessens, but it is not kosher, because it contains both meat and cheese. Frankie understood this cross-pollination on a material level, a gut level. "The butcher, the baker, the grocer, the clerk are secretly unhappy men *because* the butcher, the baker, the grocer, the clerk get paid for what they do but no *applause*! They'd gladly bid their dreary jobs *goodbye* for anything theatrical and

why?" Frankie's asking, she pushes her finger into the tabletop like the why is trying to sneak away but—snap—she got it, wriggling under her finger. Roz was there and Sid Stein was there, wriggling around like the why, chewing at her cheek they had coffee, some more. "When I was a kid I used to deliver copies of the anarchist paper" Frankie told them. She spoke like she was a friend of their fathers, a guy who'd lived you understand that don't you? she tried to say, I'm sitting you on my knee and I'm telling you about how I was the child of anarchist Jews etc etc. This image I'm painting, how I'm big enough to sit in a chair and invite you up on my knee and have you listen or to feel how it feels to have the weight of someone on your knee, to fill up a chair, I'm telling you it to be bigger than I am to paint me as big as I feel. I'm desperate to be a man. I don't mean that exactly but that's the only way I can explain it. So sometimes I do the worst bits of being a man just to feel like one, I tell stories about myself and keep speaking whether you're listening or not. I clear my throat sometimes when I don't need to. I have a sweet voice, really, like lots of boys do. I can sing, of course, I do. Anyway I haven't seen my father since I was twenty-one and I'm a little older now. Because he saw me kissing Lily. That's how Frankie started speaking when she said: "When I was a kid I used to deliver copies of the anarchist paper." When she said: "I thought about girls all the time. I thought about them like all of Tevye's daughters, Chava and her sisters, I thought about which of them I'd marry, I thought about my place as one of Tevye the Dairyman's Modern Children, I thought of forming a movement under that name for Jews who understood implicitly the role of the Reuben sandwich in the Jewish immigrant's experience of America. Now Tevye might condone modern love" she placed her finger on the table again "he might even shrug his shoulders at revolution with its crazy what's yours is mine, what's mine is yours but he will never condone apostasy" prod, prod "for the essence of Tevye is his religion, it is his chief raison d'etre, the condition of his survival and if he condoned his daughter's apostasy he would become something very much less than Tevye." Frankie took her finger off the tabletop and it hovered in the air. "The irony of it is that Tevye would understand exactly that butch is the condition of my survival" both hands to her chest, elbows out on the table leaning into them, into Sammy into Roz into Sid Stein "that if I wasn't I would be something very much less than I am." Then Roz says "The irony is that the condition of our survival is also the condition of our being hunted." "Exactly!" Frankie points at Roz "which is both the condition of Tevye's survival and the condition that his home and family be driven out of town, out of the country, out to here, to give birth to me and for me to have a condition of my own, one thing I will not falter on which I think actually is what we talk about when we talk about *tradition*!" Frankie's on a roll and places her palms on the table now really leaning in and Roz rolls her eyes because she is a daughter "Different to be a butcher's daughter" Roz says. "Than a butch!" says Sid Stein and they laugh and Frankie says "Different to be anybody's daughter! But somehow we feel the same don't we?" "Somehow" "Don't we?" Frankie says "maybe my father would understand exactly how it feels to want to wear a suit and tie, no, no my father never wanted to wear a suit, an anarchist shouldn't have to wear a suit he would say, a man must wear what best befits him and it must be a coat only if every man has a coat, but what I mean is my father was a good man, not a man who wore a suit." But I am that type of man, Frankie thought, she thought I like to wear a suit, she thought I like it best when the suit gets scruffy and it does. I like a suit worn like a pair of pajamas. I don't want you to imagine my body under my suit. I want you to look at me and see just that my body is a suit, you understand? Just that it is. When Teddy shows up it was pushing 4 a.m. Teddy in his brown suit and cream shirt with the collar loose and a tie rolled up in his inside pocket, looking like he'd just done overtime at the office, his hair still slick but a little off. Teddy sat down at the counter on his own and Laur saw him from across the room where she was sat by herself in a booth with an empty cup thinking maybe she'd get going. The sun hit the base of the sky and the pale pink outside hit the pale pink inside and painted them all in pale pink. In the soft smell of salt beef Teddy sat at the counter and took a bite of his sandwich. Laur clapped him on the shoulder, "Hey boss, need someone to finish that for you?" Teddy pushed his plate towards Laur and she sat down on the stool next to him. "Get yourself a girl tonight Ted?" "Thought I'd just head home to the one I got" "But not yet right?" "She'll be sleeping anyway and I can eat a sandwich and wake her up or I can eat a sandwich and let her sleep." Laur took a bite out of the sandwich and Teddy cringed like someone had taken a bite out of his arm. It didn't make sense to call Teddy a she so no one did, not cashiers or bartenders, not even his boss. "I guess I pass" Teddy'd said to his wife one night "shouldn't I do something more than that?" Teddy had shrugged so much he thought he'd be buried doing it or maybe if he did something good they'd erect a statue of him like that in stone and he shuddered thinking his dead body would be just as much like stone as his live one. Teddy was an awful husband if what it meant to be a husband was to be faithful, but Teddy thought what it meant to be a husband was to stick around which was different "You understand?" Teddy asked Laur hoping she would. "I could understand a little clearer" Laur said. "I'm not gonna leave her, I can't imagine my life without her I'm y'know, *stuck to her*" he said "but *faithful*" he shrugged like all the photos of him. "A person" he began again trying to get it straight "*faith*" he said "I mean" arms up and open "I mean who's got any left?" Laur pushed her knees against the counter and rocked onto the back legs of the stool. She rubbed her hand along her chin "Don't you love her more than the others Ted?" "Loves the sticky stuff kid" "Yeah" Laur thought about it, a mouthful of sandwich. "Yeah, it'll getcha" she said.

LILY

When Francesca Gold was only sixteen her father whose name was Asha Gold and who was a poet found a poem she had written in the tradition of her father the Yiddish poet. Francesca was the second generation of Yiddish anarchists in New York. She was a Goldman Baby that's what they called the children of the Yiddish anarchists: a *Goldman Baby*. The poem read

> Fucking girls Oh amerika
> Is the greatest freedom yet
> Did my people know
> Such a freedom we'd beget?
> MOTHER RUSSIA she called me
> Every time I kissed her
> Now I know that girls aren't just
> Your mother or your sister.

Her father brushed his last flop of hair back from his forehead and left his hand there. Oh Francesca, he said. That night Asha went to the bar, his hand still on his forehead. "Oh Saul I have a new burden." It was Oh everything, Oh America, Oh Saul, Oh Francesca, Oh boy Oh boy it was easy to be a poet when your natural inclination was for everything to start with a great unburdening *Oh*. It made everything erotic for Francesca from an early age, every exclamation, every newly released round cereal, every doughnut, every other poem, every prayer though she grew up without them and her own voice at a certain point said *Oh*. "Oh Saul I have a new burden" "What burden Asha? Come, take your hand off your forehead" and Saul reached round to his friend and pulled at his wrist and Asha's hand fell into his lap, upwards and open as if he held something very heavy. "I have found something other than the oppression of man that I cannot tolerate, that I cannot live with, that I know in my heart, as surely as I know I cannot condone anything but freedom, that I will never accept." Asha pushed his shirt sleeves further up his arms. The last of his hair flopped in his eyes as he hung his head. He was a good man. He was an anarchist who had known the support of so many people without question or condition and given freely his time, his money, his care in return. They had done it because they were building a new society, one without law and therefore based solely on trust, one where each man was free to act as each man wished to act so long as the actions of no man impinged upon the actions of no other

31

man's. It was a riddle he loved, one he had devoted his life to solving. He walked home in the dark hoping someone would jump him and he could punch and grab at them. It'd been such a long time since he'd fought. He wanted to kick his legs and twist to feel the resistance he had always spoken of to feel it really pulling at you and you really tugging at it. He was a lean man, a twisty kind of wiggly man. Slippery and soft like an otter. Asha never spoke to Frankie about the poem he found, or about how one Friday night he watched as she kissed Daniel's daughter Lily goodbye. He had thought it looked like a wonderful kiss, that Francesca had looked exactly like a man and Lily exactly like a woman, though neither of them were either, not to him. They had looked like movie stars, Asha thought, kissing like that.

[A Friday Night in the Past: Yiddish Anarchist Teenagers in Love] At thirteen Jews turn into men but if you do not intend to become a man then you have to choose an age at which to become something else. At sixteen Lily thought she would like to a be a woman. Lily knew that she was living in a man's world: all of the lightbulbs lemonade letterpresses envelopes lion's dens hotel lobbies liquor licorice liberty life all of it Lily understood would be forfeited and she dropped it with glee like luggage she didn't need to

32

carry anymore because she had arrived [Thunk] Lily left it all behind and imagined a future with Frankie. They'd imagined futures, of course, since they were children they had sat in anarchist groups imagining futures, living in the hope that very soon the pot will boil over, as they say, the sun will rise and everything become bright and they will all roll up their sleeves and get to work to turn the world upside down yes! Yes! Yes! Yeah Lily had heard about the future, but she'd chosen her own, the way children do. She had chosen a future with a capital F. Frankie's Fridays were for Friday meetings On Fridays Frankie's family and friends packed into living rooms listening (with Lily) to speakers from Philadelphia to France quoting Fourier on "the four affective passions tending to form the four groups of friendship." On Fridays Frankie rolled her sleeves up ready and kept her cigarettes in her back pocket and her lighter in her top pocket and her pencil behind her ear like everybody else. But more and more Frankie and Lily left early. In Lily's bedroom Frankie fidgets on the bed feeling guilty for spending her Friday night with only Lily. Though it never felt so different to Frankie to be alone with Lily than it felt to be waiting with the rest of them in the living room for the pot to overflow. Frankie and Lily had spent their Fridays at meetings forever "Our whole lives" Lily said "don't you think we could skip one?" Frankie undid her top button and rolled up her sleeves. Lily took the lighter from her top pocket and lit a cigarette. Among other things, Frankie and Lily had fallen in love. "We're Goldman Babies" Frankie said "You more than me". "Me?" "Yeah you, you're a real revolutionary" and Lily tweaked the peak of Frankie's cap and brushed down her collar "not like me. *Frankie Gold the Goldman Baby*" Lily said, a little jet plane slipping out from between her lips and skywriting in pink steam Frankie Gold the Goldman Baby spelled out in the air, the steam settling over their heads, turning to grey and coming away from itself like meat off a bone. "How dyu get to be such a boy anyway?" Lily ran her finger along Frankie's jaw and rested it in the dip of her chin "The trick's to slick your hair back instead of forward" Frankie said "It only makes me look like a ballerina to slick my hair back, it makes you look like Sal Marino" "He's Italian" Lily shrugged "So" she said "we're all from somewhere." Lying with her head in Lily's lap Frankie opened her mouth and Lily put her fist inside it "You messin with my gal, buster?" she said and through Lily's fist Frankie sounded "Nuh-uh" "Keep your hands off my Lilian, or I'll serve you up my finest fist sandwich, Frankie Gold." When Frankie was with Lily her clothes fit right and her arms swung and slung their jacket over their shoulder and her smart shoes walked about. I have often walked down this street before but the pavement always stayed beneath my feet before all at once am I several stories high knowing I'm on the street where you live. Asha had spent all the rest of his life after the death of his wife still loving her. He spoke about her like a fine dinner he had been eating continuously up until the point of her death. He didn't lose his spirit, he didn't stop living because she did, he simply kept loving her as if she were alive, didn't shift to a dead kind of love it was always an alive sort even though there wasn't anything there to love and that's how Frankie had learnt to love, the way a man loves a dead woman, or an anarchist loves anarchism. The way perfect things are perfect. At sixteen Frankie and Lillian were alive for one another. "Let's not say we'll die for anything" Lily falls into Frankie's arms "for the cause or for each other, let's say we will live for it. For it all and most of all for each other." But when Frankie left, Lily didn't go. For Frankie the bars were a natural progression from the living room floors of their childhood among the comrades of their fathers. At the bar Frankie still rolled her sleeves up ready and kept her cigarettes in her back pocket and her lighter in her top pocket and her pencil behind her ear only now she did it how a butch does it, not how an anarchist does. "Some scene" Lily huffed. She didn't want the same, not the same as Frankie and not the same as before. It was Sammy who went with, Frankie Gold's own Sammy Silver who'd had her own anarchist father and sat on the carpet with Lily and Frankie on Friday nights. Whose parents had eaten dinners together and left them to play and to write their own childish anarchist papers, that same Sammy who'd tried to kiss Frankie just to try it when they were only kids, younger than ten and who'd grown up to be a similar shape to Frankie, and Sam had idolized Frankie and Frankie loved Sam. And now, ladies and gentlemen: *Sammy Silver and Frankie Gold.*

[A Friday Night in the Here and Now] Frankie leant forward onto the deli table. "He thought I was anathema, he couldn't believe it" "Believe it?" Sid asked. "Believe it!" Frankie said. "My father believed it alright" said Roz "in a you better believe it kinda way." Frankie's shaking her head. "He just" shake "he couldn't even conceive of it, a poet! He couldn't imagine it!" slaps the palm of her hand on the table with the coffee cups "belief? What a worm" slam, her hand with the coffee and the ashtray and the sugar pot together, a group of things. "He's the unbelievable one Frank" Sid said "you don't need him" "Need him?" Frankie fell back into her seat, winded "I—I'm—" Need him? she thought of all the other things she needed and tried to put her father in a list with them—a new pair of shoes, a loaf of bread. Frankie could cry. Sammy said something to stop her and Sid liked the sound of it because it sounded like it was drawing something to a close. Sid wanted to get going. Not just now all the time. Sid was hoping they'd be invited back to Sam and Frankie's and that Frankie would sing. She loved it when Frankie sang. Not because it was Frankie but because it was singing. Sid Stein wasn't a musician, couldn't hold a tune but loved music like like like women. Sid Stein had a gentle double chin and very dark hair which was thick and curly and short and greased through slick and shiny. She wore a black t shirt and a black denim jacket and black jeans and her gentle double chin looked like the gentle tits she bundled into her clothes every day like they were feet in her shoes. Sid Stein had come from Jersey from a small enclave of Polish Jews there and she had not grown up an anarchist but a Zionist whose family had missed the boat and so ended up to her mother's dismay in New Jersey. "At least we're not dead" her father would say, and her mother would slam about and cling and clang and say "I'd rather a pogrom!" in her thick Polish voice, with the stress on the "grom" saying the word like a sneeze ha-*choo* or po-*grom*. Sid Stein had a full lower lip and her mouth hung slightly open from the weight of it. Sid had stuffed her crotch with socks since she could remember. She didn't remember conceiving of the idea just remembered seeing socks and wanting to stuff them in her pants. She still stuffed her crotch, with all different stuff depending on who she was seeing and where she was going and whether she hoped to take her pants off in front them. And then made sure she balled up expensive or at least clean socks. Sid worked in a hot dog factory between Jersey and the city and lived at home with her mother and father but was hardly there. The factory made two types of franks, kosher franks and regular. Both were just beef and beef parts but at the end of one production line a rabbi came to bless the jars and on the other line the franks just went on their way unblessed. Straight to hell. "We don't believe in hell, Gloria" her father would say, quietly, as her mother crashed about "Well whaddaya call this?" she'd yell back at him "I'd rather—" "I know, I know" her father would say "the po*grom*." So little Sid Stein with her stuffed socked crotch went out into Jersey from a young age and kissed girls under the boardwalk. "Are we gonna get going?" Sid said. She wished she'd ended up with the meatheads instead of the anarchists who were always thinking and discussing, even when they joined in the bar brawls they'd be discussing it at one end or the other sometimes whilst it was happening yadda yadda yadda Sid'd rather the meatheads. They hardly spoke but you could tell they had big ideas or why'd they be in the bars? It's not that Sid didn't believe in anarchy, Sid did. Sid believed in anarchy. Anarchism was the second greatest thing she'd learnt about in her whole life. Frankie'd taught her about anarchism, she didn't know she was an anarchist until she met Frankie, she'd thought she was only a Jew. Only it was that Sid wasn't a thinker she was a doer! And anarchism allowed for that, in anarchism they called it "the deed" which Sid sniggered at because that's what her mother called sex when she sat her down to talk about it. "Don't let me catch you doing *the deed*" she'd said, but Sid hadn't listened. The deed was what Sid lived for. You needed to find stuff to live for when you were butch. That was something Sid had thought a little about. Because there wasn't anything. Nothing laid out, really, not like you were a hot dog who was meant for a jar or even a bun, being butch wasn't like that. It was the deed Sid did! Sid did a lot of doing as much doing as she could (do). Sid was a good anarchist. Sid'd left the house wearing double layers of socks and then when the coast was clear had slipped off her shoes and one layer of socks and balled them together and slipped them down into her underwear. Sid was a kid then and a kid now. She'd picked up her first girl at thirteen years old which is the perfect time for a girl to pick up a girl if Sid was a girl which she didn't give two fucks about. Frankie read aloud to her sat in her apartment, "Come round Sid I'll read you it over dinner." And Sid'd bring her a jar of hot dogs, the kosher ones just out of habit and the jar'd sit on the side until the next time she was round. "For the revolution" she'd say, as she handed them over. It was a Kropotkin joke, she was very proud of that, and Frankie'd give her a smile. Frankie'd be wearing slippers and her coat with its collar up because it was winter and her apartment was freezing cold and maybe Sammy'd come home. Hi Sidney, Hey Sam. Sammy in a light denim jacket and light denim jeans and a cream-colored shirt and a big flop of her hair in her eyes with her head hung forward so it never wasn't. Frankie'd stood in front of Sammy a bunch of times acting like a mirror "How'd I look?" she'd asked and Frankie would move her hair a little to the left and tug at her jacket a little to square it just right. And Sammy had done the same "How'd I look?" Frankie'd asked and Sammy would say "Like a slouch." "For the revolution" Sid said, putting the jar on the counter. "When comes the revolution and how will it announce its coming?" Frankie said, using her arms. "Should have called it 'The Conquest of the Hot Dog Factory' then I'm your guy" Frankie clapped her hand on Sid's shoulder and showed her to a seat. "It can be the conquest of the hot dog factory Sid" "I'm working on it" "Yeah? Yeah how's it going over there, are the boys listening to you?" "The boys? No" "The bosses?" "Even less" "You have to make your voice heard in that union Sidney" said Frankie. "Yes boss" said Sid. Anyway when she was thirteen she'd been sitting on the edge of the pier one night when it was warm with her shoes off and she'd seen a bunch of girls below her on the beach, the girls must have been older because from there Sid could see right down their shirts and Sid didn't have tits yet, just a sweet little belly and puppy bulges at her biceps which she could tense and turn into muscles. She was wearing blue jeans and a t shirt her dad had bought her on a trip to Coney Island which said *papa loves you* on it. Her hair was long and thick and black down to her shoulders and she pushed it back behind her ears and stuck a baseball cap over the top of it, she looked like a wise guy. But a Jewish one, with light skin almost blue even in summer with her big lip hanging down. She let a pebble drop into the group of girls and they looked up. Hey! And she laughed and the girls acted like they were mad, who me? she said standing up pointing at her chest acting all what's the big idea. She'd caught the eye especially of this Irish looking girl, or something different, she didn't know what people looked like whatever, she wasn't a Jew she knew that. Took a swagger down to where the girls were. "Hey you, you always throw stones?" "Only at pretty girls." And that was it. In the dark on the beach under the pier Sid had pushed her sock-stuffed crotch into the thigh of that Irish girl or whatever and she'd kissed her and kissed her and kissed her. The deed. That was what Sid Stein thought about.

Frequently Sid imagined lobbing jars of hot dogs like baseballs across the factory at the foreman's head and jumping up onto the conveyor belt her hands on her hips and her legs apart grabbing the foreman by the collar and dragging him round slowly but not slowly enough like the pace of the conveyor belt which never let you relax just kept you going shooting past and saying: "Are you kosher Stanley?" And he'd squeal "What! what get the fuck off me" and wriggle but her hand'd be on his collar and he'd be pulled along still as she made her way round and round the factory on the belt "I can't hear you Stanley but you better be kosher or we can't can you here, not on this belt so I'll ask again *Stan* are you blessable or what? Is the good rabbi here gonna be able to bless the filth off you or are you too filthy for that Stanley? You better not be or we ain't gonna be able to can you here boss not on this belt" "I am I am!" Stan would cry.

FRIDAY NIGHT

[That's Butch Night Out! First, Dinner at Marg's]
"No one else likes dykes why should I" Marg says.
Groan. Teddy says "Have we got to talk about it
over eating Marg? It's making the beef tough" *mmm
hmm*. "Sorry Ted let's talk about baseball" losing at
baseball/winning at baseball yadda yadda. At tables
in America the food did the talking Mr. Peanut etc
talking hot dogs talking cookies talking oranges,
talking onions. Assimilation was to do with how
quickly the foods you brought with you grew legs and
started tap dancing. Tap-dancing tacos, tap-dancing gherkins yes definitely. Tap-dancing forks with
swirls of spaghetti hair flirting with broad-shouldered
pizza slices and making eyes at sauce bottles. Marg
pushed her chair back from the table and the mustard teetered in its jar. "Anything from the fridge?"
"Shouldn't we get going?" said Vic. Laur was sitting
at the other end of the table. They'd caught eyes a
few times. It was easier than they thought to be butch

together. It wasn't so different from being butch to a femme when anyway you were always being butch for somebody else. That's not it exactly, it was that you were butch and that was that but the poses and fronts, the moves, that was the way you were butch for other people. It was the way the butchness came out of your body. Maybe it'd be through your eyes, or your scent, or the way you danced. There are all sorts of ways the body lets the inside of it leak out and Vic and all the others wanted it to leak out butch. Suzy came out of the kitchen and sat on Marg's knee. Marg looked like a real sleaze. Her big body holding onto this other body as if she owned it, but Suzy loved Marg and her big body and how it held her as if she wasn't her own anymore. Marg was like a steam train unable to let off enough steam. Suzy was a tall glass of water. They lived with Marg's parents. The house had two floors and her parents spent their days on the top while below them Marg and Suzy set up house together. They have each other, Marg always said about her parents, Marg was straight like that. That was the model. Suzy read to Marg's father and made the house fresh for Marg's mother and Marg. "How do you put up with her Suzy?" Laur asked being silly. "Haven't you ever lived with somebody Laur?" "Sure" she hadn't "Well when it gets to be putting up with somebody instead of getting along with them didn't you move out?" "Sure" "I

44

don't have anything to put up with. It's simple as that" "See?" Marg said being silly "What about her jokes?" Teddy put in and they all laughed haw haw. Teddy's hair wouldn't stay slicked back anymore, and his collars weren't stiff. Teddy looked good of course, like a man who has come home from work looks good only Teddy got home from work and got into a suit not out of it. He'd never found a job that'd let him wear one, he'd barely found a job. Laur thought Teddy was starting to look too much like an animal. It was hard to see the humanity in him. Laur thought about aliens. She'd thought about aliens a lot since talking with Vic. It was easier than they thought to be butch together. It wasn't so different. Vic and Laur had turned up together to Marg's "Where's the bike Vic?" Marg'd asked at the door "You wanna pay for the gas?" she'd replied. "Only if the engine comes free" "Well it doesn't" "Hey wanna get the subway fee instead Margy?" Laur'd clapped Marg on the back and gone in, asking "How are ya Marg? How's mama and papa?" avoiding having to say how she'd met Vic at the steps down to the subway, two slick looking bouncing things, bouncy looking slick two, dressed almost exactly the same in motorcycle jackets and blue jeans and crisp white t shirts. But they looked different even dressed the same Vic looked solid and flat like a poster on a teenager's bedroom wall and Laur looked liquid and brighter like a pack of gum. On the subway they sat next to one another which they might not have done if anyone else had been there but no one was Vic said "How was work?" and Laur said "You asking questions now?" "Yeah, about you." Laur said "I didn't get any scraps" "No scraps! What's a dishwasher in the game for?" "Exactly! It's 'cause I'm not Italian" "Aren't you?" "Who cares! I washed all the dishes can't they give me a slice of something?" "Well Marg will feed you" "You hungry?" Vic shrugged. "Oh yeah?" Laur shoved her on the arm "what's that growling then?" They'd had a fight one night. All the hanging around together what was it meant to end in some kind of conversation? Some kind of kiss? Some kind of proposal? They'd been at a bar, met up on a quiet night somewhere they didn't go to much but still they knew the bartender. Drank beers and some whiskey and chatted across a booth table ignoring anyone else that came in when maybe in any other situation they'd have been keeping an eye out. Vic had told a story about being a kid and Laur'd just listened. "Lessgo" Laur'd said, seeing Vic go past it, her eyelids heavy and her jaw all slack. Laur'd dragged her out onto the street and the fresh air had straightened them both up a little, they walked a while in the same direction. "Fancy a brawl V?" Laur said already bouncing on her toes like a boxer. "Knock it off" Vic'd laughed. "Go on Vic I fancy a fight" foot to foot bounce bounce, a sharp little jab under Vic's chin. "Watch it" jab and Vic'd taken the bait, given a little jab back and they'd ended up tugging at each other's jackets and making a ruckus in the street but no one much bothered to look at two young greasy things bashing each other about in the street, not much. Ended up with a split lip each maybe "Alright alright get off me will ya?" Vic pushing Laur off her and Laur'd been lost in it, like she always got lost in a fight. Laur was all red in the face and they'd gotten scrappy kinds of dirt stains on their jeans. Vic had given her one last shove and said "Go to hell" walking away. And she'd heard Laur laughing like she'd lost her senses behind her, still getting her breath back. "Fuck you Vic" she yelled back at her, already across the street.

Only Lily *did* go to the bars sometimes, where else could she go! If Frankie didn't know then Sammy knew because of the BOP which Lily had told Sammy about having heard about it through the other Sammy. Sammy had heard that Lily had fallen for this other Sammy one night after seeing her play in a bar uptown and, learning that this fresh Sammy played there every Friday went most Fridays to watch Sammy play, *fresh*. But Sammy didn't ask much about it, if she knew too much she'd have to keep too much from Frankie. It was simple really that Frankie was tied to Lily like people get tied to things that go badly. Lily wasn't tied to Frankie in that same way because Lily's mother and father didn't hurt Lily at the moment she should've been growing and so leave her short of being able to. Which is what Frankie's father had done when he chose to let her leave and worst of all used anarchism to justify it, used autonomy "What about mutual aid?" Frankie'd said, as Asha sat looking at his hands fiddling with nothing on the table like it always was. Frankie'd stood with her bag in her hand and her coat and cap and Asha'd said "You're free to leave" and then just skipped the lecture and mumbled ". . . autonomy . . ." "What about mutual aid?" "We're not helping each other anymore" Asha'd said "I never knew there was a certain amount of autonomy I could have before it turned into exile, you never told me that" "Francesca" "What, did you teach me about freedom my whole life 'cause you knew one day I'd be out on my own?" "Of course I did!" Managing to look up and seeing her, looking down again and asking "do you think I thought you'd be with me forever?" "I thought I could come back" "I'm telling you do whatever you want!" "But not here" "I never said that" "Said? You've barely spoken to me. This is the most we've said to each other since I told you!" "I'm not trying to stop you and that's all I can do." And in that way Asha *had stopped* Frankie, that's what Sammy thought, he hadn't stopped her from leaving but he'd stopped her from being ok, because people who are ok are people whose fathers love them and whose mothers are alive, and Frankie needed at least one of them didn't she? Imagine being so much like somebody who didn't want to even eat their breakfast by you, looking like somebody who couldn't bear to look at you. The bars were full of it of course and that's why you didn't make eye contact with anybody apart from the girl you wanted to go with, then you looked at them straight in the eyes and they looked nothing like you. That was what was sexy about girls, that they looked nothing like you. And Lily looked at her latest Sammy like that, like a girl looks at a boy. Louis' place had little round tables like a club not booths like a bar, and people sat together like frogs on lily pads. Sammy had noticed Lily too "You need a drink?" "Sure" "Did you arrive in time?" "For what?" "For the music" "I arrived in time" all this while Sammy's trying to lick her lips and Lily's trying to touch her neck and their eyes are drawing loops around each other. Lily and her fresh Sammy didn't have anything official going on, it was more a Friday night arrangement, but wasn't that more solid than an any-night-of-the-week-type arrangement? Every Friday Sammy played and every Friday Lily turned up. "You never told me you were an anarchist" "Didn't I?" Lily said "I would've remembered" "Why?" "Because not everybody is an anarchist" "We're always recruiting" "Not me, you didn't even mention it" "You never asked" "I never thought to" "Doesn't it show?" Sammy looked at Lily and thought maybe it did "I don't know what I'm looking for" "Oh?" "What do I look like to you?" "A stud" "You say that like it's a bad thing" "I don't mean to" "Oh?" "I only say it like it's a fact" "It is" "I know that, but you don't know what I look like" "I don't know what an anarchist looks like so I don't know if you look like one" "Well everybody says I look like my grandmother and she was an anarchist." They're at one of those little round tables. "Sammy Silver came to the BOP last week that's all" "Alone?" Lily asked "Yeah, said you'd sent her and that you two are old friends" "We are." The BOP was set up by a cohort of butch piano players who made their living predominantly in gay bars. Until Sammy Silver turned up it was solely Black butches who'd learned lessons from their communist fathers. Their founding principles were equal pay for all players, regardless of race and regardless of renown. Following that, equal access for all piano players to a piano to practice on in order to encourage the best level of piano playing among homosexuals so as to compete against heterosexual piano players. Following that, the communization of resources—distribution of song sheets, audition details, as well as the encouragement of musical collaboration on original music. Sammy Silver hadn't heard about it until Lily had said "How come you don't go to the BOP?" "I don't know about it" "It's the union for butch piano players they run it out of Louis' place you play there don't you?" "Sometimes" "Louis's a part of it, and Sammy who plays, you've met her" "Maybe" Lily and her old Sammy (good old Sammy) are chatting on the phone: "Hello" "Hello Sammy" "Did you call for me?" "No I called for my father" it's the office phone "Shall I get him" "Sure—Sammy" "Yes" "How come you don't go to the BOP?" "I don't know about it" "It's the union for butch piano players they run it out of Louis' place you play there don't you?" "Sometimes" "Louis's a part of it, and Sammy who plays, you've met her" "Maybe" "It's every two weeks on Mondays after hours" "Are you going to be there?" "Why would I be at butch piano players union Sam?" "I don't know, for numbers?" "I've got enough phone numbers." "I meant the union, needs numbers they all do" "It's doing fine, you'll be an asset of course." "Do they need a printer?" "Who doesn't. Sammy is my father there or not?" "I'll get him now."

[After Dinner at Marg's] Meanwhile it's a busy night and everybody's shouting. Dinner was fine nothing exciting and they'd all felt like they wanted to get going. They'd thanked Suzy on the way out getting their coats after scraping their plates saying "You sure you're not coming?" "I'm sure" and Marg had kissed her and she'd pushed her hands through Marg's hair to set it back in place then wiped the grease off on the tops of her jeans and she'd smoked a cigarette in the kitchen and watched them all Marg and Laur and Vic and Teddy walk off down the street like clowns pouring out of a clown car. Like notes on a stave. Like a round of applause. They trickled down into the basement bar and split up looking for something different. The music made the same sound the glasses and bottles made. The jukebox made eyes at everybody. "Tell me I'm dreaming" somebody said. "Don't look now but" somebody said. "You and me both" somebody said. "You care about fucking any more Teddy?" Laur said "What part?" said Teddy "The getting to part" "You're asking if I wanna fuck anymore?" "Sure, maybe" "What else do you expect me to do?" "You call that caring?" "I care as much as I'd rather be doing it than doing my laundry or queuing at the post office. Or talking to you" "Well I care about it like I'm scared half of me will disappear if don't keep filling it with somebody else." Laur drunk the rest of her beer down and hopped off her stool "It makes my knees freeze" touches her knees "it makes my back crack" puts her hands on her hips "it makes my liver quiver" shakes her shoulders like she's cold "boogaloo boogaloo I gotta do it just for you, boogaloo" puts her finger to her chin like a girl. Then she combs her hair back in place, raps a cigarette pack on the back of her hand and lights a cigarette. "Two halves don't always make a whole, chops" "I'm pretty sure they do *chops*" sits back down on the bar stool, one leg up on the rung so she can bounce her knee to the music "Well I'm telling you they don't, sometimes they make a mess and that's all they make" "I'm already a mess Ted" "Yeah well at least you're only half a mess, and you know what you get when you find another half?" "A whole mess" "A whole mess, a whole lotta mess. I'd rather have half" "So you don't care about fucking" "More like I don't fucking care." Music starts and everything's busy again. Teddy just merges into the scene and Laur looks about. Blur, blur. "Keep the change" somebody says "You betcha" someone's saying "What'll it be?" somebody asks—Ah there you are!— Laur spots Vic through the crowd and makes her way to her, tipping her hips about to fit through all the people, her arms up high to keep her balance holding her beer bottle by the neck above everybody's heads slug slug, trying to reach her. Tapping on her shoulder and finding some place to lean. "You care about fucking Vic?" Vic thought it through. Do I care about fucking? At first her thinking was well what the hell am I doing here if I don't? and she thought of all the other places she could be instead, that didn't stink of old beer and cigarettes and didn't take twenty minutes

53

for your eyes to adjust to the darkness before you saw that there weren't any spare tables anyway and you'd be standing the whole night waiting. Waiting for what? It wasn't only fucking she was here for of course, it was a bunch of things, but anyway even if it was only fucking wasn't that enough, fucking was worthy of waiting for wasn't it? Fucking was alright, nothing bad about it, made you feel good mostly. It was the care bit she got stuck on. "It's not so much I care about it" she said her voice low and mumbling grinding her back teeth and saying "more that I'm careful about it" "I'm careless with it, could care less about it" "What you wanna be alone the rest of these nights?" "The opposite, I could care less who I'm with as long as I'm not alone all these nights. I couldn't care less if my mother knew her. Not fucking's the nightmare Vic, hell I'd be homeless most of the time if I didn't anyway. Hey you know how people hide things under the bed? under the mattress maybe like a dirty book or a box of something you're ashamed of?" "Sure" "Where've I been hiding things if I never had a bed?" "You got something needs hiding?" "Don't I look like I do?" Vic laughed and said "What's the opposite of hiding?" "I dunno" "Well, you look like that" Laur laughed "Yeah. I suppose we both of us look more like telling. Still I'd like to have something under the mattress" "Cash" "Sure or some picture of somebody" "Wouldn't you rather have a wall for that?" "Nah." Laur only wanted a bed. Marg is headed their way. Spinning slowly off the dance floor, the needle lifted off her gently and waiting impatiently to drop again, always ready to play like a dog with its head cocked, waiting for Marg to put a penny in the slot again let's play, let's play. Gimme a break! Marg bats the jukebox away. Heads to the bar. [Vic's outta there] Marg claps Laur on the back and leans where Vic was leaning. "You care about fucking Marg?" Laur's asking. "Haven't you got any better language for it than that?" "I got plenty you if wanna hear it—" "No" " Boogaloo, a roll in the hay, a lady's lunch, the pepper grinder, making it, shaking it, whoopee—" "I get it I get it at least they don't sound like things you'd do to somebody you hated" "You might" "It's compli- cated" "Well do you care about it?" "Of course I do" Marg squared her shoulders and moved the knot in her tie so it was straight "you gotta care about it otherwise you never get it and what's the point of this life we're living without the feel of a woman?" Marg said things like "the feel of a woman" because Marg was aging out of this scene, out of this bar with its music she was starting not to like and the clothes she didn't feel right wearing. The kids now looked shiny and scruffy like race cars, all the kids in the bar when Marg had showed up had looked more like hearses, too big and too empty but sleek and smart like they respected something. She didn't know what you could fit in these kids, these kids looked empty too but unfillable. Laur was the hungriest kid she'd ever fed. She liked Laur, Laur was happy and you didn't see that much. "You think Suzy wants me to talk about boogaloo with a punk like you?" "Don't you come to the bars to talk to guys like me?" Marg came to bars out of habit. "Do guys like you cover the tab?" "Not yet they don't" "You got plans?" "I got nothing" "Yeah well" Marg rolled her neck and it cracked and she slugged Laur on the shoulder "I do" "Looking to dance tonight?" "Now if you ask do I care about dancing I do. No doubt about it, sure I can dance at home with Suzy we do too, but I like watching people dance and this is the only place for it. A whole dance floor of people holding each other and hearing the same music, I like to see that Laur, don't you?" "Sure" Marg was soppy in a way guys weren't anymore. Laur thought the older you got the soppier you got, your roots were deeper in the earth and they were soaking up more than the kids whose roots were just in the dust, dug in so shallow it barely kept them standing. The newer kids were floppier, they were bendier like metal heated up and the older guys with their roots down deep got all soppy but they wouldn't budge, soft and solid at the same time. Soft in all the wrong places, Laur thought. Marg was like a gorilla yeah, just like a gorilla the way that seeing a picture of a gorilla makes you wanna cry because of the way it looks just like you and just like an animal all at the same time.

SOME FRIDAY

"Did you ever see the playbill for Doris Day doing Secret Love from Calamity Jane?" [Cue Sammy Silver on piano] Frankie spoke to the audience in a voice not quite like her speaking voice and a voice not quite like her singing voice, but the voice that came out when the two voices met. "It doesn't get much gayer than that." The crowd laughs, Sammy plays. "Of course I went to see it!" Frankie said, and they laugh and raise their glasses, "though I'm not much of a Calamity Jane" and she straightened her tie with her free hand, holding the microphone in the other, walking along the front of the stage "no, ladies and gentlemen I'm afraid I'm more of a" Sammy's piano in the background "Bill Hickok" laugh "only without the . . . well, you understand" big laugh "which I suppose just makes me a hick." Haw haw haw. Frankie's facing her feet but her eyes are looking up at the audience like she's the boy and they're the girl. And

Sammy's playing the opening bars over and over to Secret Love from Calamity Jane, as if music was always playing when Frankie spoke. *Once I had a secret love cheer that lived within the heart of me. All too soon my secret love became impatient to be free* cheer cheer! *so I told a friendly star the way that dreamers often do. Just how wonderful you are and why I'm so in love with you* shout *it! Now I shout it! From the highest hills, even told the golden daffodils, at last my heart's an open dooooor* cheer cheer! *and my secret loves no secret a-ny-more.* Applause. Hey! I know you! Yeah? Yeah I've seen you! You have? Seen you play! That's me. You've got rhythm! I've got music. And Sammy lets Frankie know "I'm gonna take off" puts on her long black coat and loosens her piano player's tie and takes her satchel full of sheet music, stands in the doorway to light up a cigarette, turns her collar up, and walks out of the bar. Until it's suddenly after hours and Frankie's still there at Louis' place, with Louis whose father was a communist "But it wasn't a family thing" "He didn't talk about it?" "No it was more like what the men did while women were washing the dishes, you know like, we'd eat dinner, we'd get up, he'd go be a communist and we'd clear the table and go to bed" "I can't imagine my father shutting up about it but then my father hates communists. Sorry" "That's ok I hate my father" "Huh" "He passed it down though" "You couldn't fight it" Frankie wondered if her father had never said a word would she have been an anarchist because of the way the air smelled in the house or the way she'd watched her parents set the table, if she'd only ever noticed the rhythm of her father's blinking eyes would she have been an anarchist? "Had to be in the house of course" Louis said "what other space did he have? Somebody's house you know and all the women in the front room making it seem like it was just women's business and then in the back all the Comintern is there growing out its beard you know, wearing its glasses." Frankie knew. There had been a brief period of Black communist and Yiddish anarchist coalition, one of those moments where history piled up and teetered in different directions. Now Louis and Frankie were friends but that wasn't the same thing. Louis wrung out her rag and Frankie sat at the bar all the chairs up on the tables and the floor smelling like mop water and no music just the zing of the jukebox turning off. "Karl Marx said the workers have nothing to lose but their chains" "Did he?" "Yeah he said that" "What an idiot" Louis starts counting the money out of the register, licks her thumb and speaks "[1 2 3 4] of all the things I could lose [5 6 7 8] the chains are the thing I think about least [1 2 3 4] I think about losing my children" shakes her head "oh fuck" loses her place starts counting again "I think about losing my *life* [2 3 4] nothing to lose but my chains [6 7 8] what a fucking sleaze" shaking her head "I don't know what I've got to lose" "You mean you don't know what you got" "I didn't know you had kids Lou" [shrug 2 3 4] "I didn't know you didn't" Frankie smiles "How many kids?" "2 kids 7 and 8 [1 2 3 4]" "I like kids kids have a lot of energy" "Yeah [2 3 4]" "Nothing to lose but their chains pah" "Ttsss [2 3 4]" "It don't mean a thing if you ain't got that swing" "Tell it to Marx." Meanwhile Sammy Silver's been with Lillian at a coffee shop. Beer bottles shuffle out the way to make room for the coffee cups. The coffee shop smells like coffee. Sammy's satchel of song sheets is down by her feet and her long black coat is on the back of the chair and she has taken off her piano player's tie. She speaks to Lily with that kind of restless energy she gets after she plays and Lily knows Sammy isn't listening anymore, she's done all her listening for the night. "Anarchism is unrequited love. It is hope without end do you know how tiring that is? And people give up you know? They give up. Not because they realize it's impossible, that they've been trying and trying to make something happen that simply can't because it can! But because they know it's *very hard*. That's all. That's it. What they are trying to make happen is very hard to make happen and that's the toss-up, to put in the effort of hope or to numb yourself so you don't have to try anymore for each other. And so yeah ok yes some people say you know what? I'll

61

just stop walking now, it's been a nice walk I've had a nice walk but I have to rest now" throw your arms up "that's it. I have to rest now" shake your head deeply very dipped, understanding. Nod. Nod. Shake. Arms. "I" look for words to say more clearly than that "I just have to!" Sammy's saying "So maybe then they're not anarchists anymore, just friends. But the difference is so slight between them!" show with your fingers the difference is slight "so slight" show "between friendship and anarchism" Sammy's said it. "Do you think all immigrants' children see their parents melting like we saw ours melt?" Lily asks her. "Ours? They haven't melted Lil, they've barely thawed out!" Laughs. It was especially funny because Lily's parents had come from Siberia. The two spoke about the tepele zup, the pot of soup. [The butches sit around a table in the deli, it's a Friday night late late, after the bars they're telling each other about each other's nights.] Roz: "I really have to get going" Frankie: "You just got here" Roz: "No you were late" Frankie: "Please Roz, who is it anyway?" Roz: "No one you know I hope" Laugh. Meanwhile everybody else is talking. Never not talking over one another. Each voice is a part of a mix that makes up the pot of soup. Roz is an onion and puts herself in the pot and then Frankie who is celery goes in and says something back to Roz and then Sidney says we're really from different meat markets Roz, I'm a frank and you're a—maybe Roz is the stock actually, the stock bone or maybe that's her father. Roz looked like Sidney but shinier, a Sid who grew up with money. Roz: "If my father knew I was hanging around with you bums he'd change the locks." She wore a white shirt but with a few more buttons undone something like a blouse and black jeans that went higher up her waist than the other butches and she was shiny, like a polished Sidney, she had a husky voice it really knocked you sideways she was really gorgeous that was it. Really the belle juive role, really, the butch belle juive. E.g. "Hey honey you going home already?" "Who's askin?" and it's the healthy-looking well-bred Roz one step away from showing this gal her gums. See these gums? she's saying, hooking her finger under her top lip. And there they are, a deep pink. *Click*—Roz leans against the bar and clicks her fingers—*click, click, click*—and there's a whisper going round: Who's that? Who's she? Seen her? Sssssshhh. Her shiny gums flash when she smiles and stock simmers on the inside of her rich as her bones and the air around her is hazy and hot and the girls watch as she appears through the steam: Roz put the butch in kosher butcher's daughter. "Roz puts the *bar* in *bar mitzvah*" Sid cracked. Roz hadn't known there'd be Jews in the bars. In this crowd everybody did their best to not know anything about anybody else. When you met another Jew at the bar the things you couldn't hide

were the exact type of things you tried to avoid telling, the stuff you were before. Really people arrived
at the bar like they just stepped off the factory belt.
They seemed to have no before or afters. No rela-
tionship to time at all. They couldn't have mothers
because that would mean they had been children,
they had been to school and kid's parties and played
in the park not just turned up here, like this. But if
being a Jew meant anything at all which it didn't not
really apart from if being a Jew meant anything, it
meant having a mother. So from the moment they'd
met—Roz and Sid Stein and Frankie and Sammy—
they had already said too much. "My mother was
part of LABTAA you know, and my father. That's
the Ladies Anti-Beef Trust Association they led the
food riots against the kosher butchers in 1902 of
course, you've heard about it" Sammy says "they had
beef with beef!" Laugh. Laugh. Frankie chimes in
says "So was my mother" eyes roll, of course "so tell
your father you're hanging around with the enemy"
"Oh, he worked that out already" says Roz. Frankie
stood up in the booth and put on the voice of her
grandmother who was an anarchist and who had lived
while she had lived despite having led a life made up
mostly of nearly dying. "The people feel very justly"
Frankie said wagging her finger doing her grandmother's voice and everyone laughing haw haw "that
they are being ground down" haw haw "by the beef

trust of the city" haw haw rolling around laughing laughing. "And they lost didn't they? Didn't they lose, I mean look at us, ground beef!" haw haw! And up at the counter something else happens and outside on the street something else happens and at the next table something else happens. Roz: "Some people never get rich" Frankie: "Some people don't want to" Roz: "Some people can't help but" Frankie: "Oh they can help it." Roz: "Is it their fault people want meat?" Frankie: "It's their fault the people need to ask them for it" Roz: "Butchery is a skill you know" Frankie: "Don't I know it, it's the finest skill in America — *butchery*—don't look too much like meat in America my friends they're just waiting to butcher you here look at me! I spend my evenings butchering songs!" Roz: "And how does a butcher afford to eat if he gives meat away instead of selling it?" Frankie: "The way we all eat" Roz: "I don't blame my father for selling meat" Frankie: "Who can blame him?" Roz: "It's like Sammy's grandfather says about shoes—" Frankie: "No it is not! Sammy's grandfather worked in a shoe factory" Roz: "—And if he didn't!" Frankie: "And if he didn't he wouldn't have shoes but that's not so for the butcher! There'd be meat without him!" Meanwhile, Lily and Sammy are in the coffee shop. Time adjusted the knot in its tie and sat up straight again. And Sammy's been talking. "Italians wanted different things out of America than the Jews did"

Sammy says. "I think the Italians are better anarchists than us" Lily says. She'd had an affair with an Italian anarchist having fallen for the way she called it *anarchismo*. This Italian anarchist had had almost exactly the same upbringing as Lily but the food they had eaten had been so vastly different that Lily was sure there was no way they could be at all similar, to sit down to such different meals and chew and swallow almost the opposite of each other Lily thought, what did the books, the reading matter? it couldn't have settled the same inside of them. Lily had forgotten after a while that her Casanova was an anarchist at all, she couldn't see it on her, not like she saw it on the Jews whose anarchism was like a layer of grease on them, like it'd come from the cooking. "Well the Italians have a lower melting point than us" Sammy says "Do they?" Lily guffaws "There are as many delis selling sandwiches as there are coffee shops aren't there?" "I don't know" Sammy says "maybe, but Yiddish doesn't melt Lil, I know it doesn't, I touch it every day typesetting" Sammy shows Lily her fingers "look" she says "it's on my goddam skin" "If the lead gets into the soup it'll poison it" Lily supposes "and that's what we want isn't it?" It wasn't strange to talk about soup like this, it was easy for Lily to understand that growing up for Sammy and for her and for Frankie and all the other Goldman Babies the atmosphere had felt overwhelmingly soup-like, which was to do with bubbling and to do with steam and heat in some way and to do with damp or wet or something and to do with big pots to do with a great carryingness somehow, this was what Lily and Sammy simply understood. Lily: "How's Frankie?" Sammy went stiff. "Frankie's fine she asks after you." Frankie didn't. How Sammy managed to live with a foot on each side of this great gulf she didn't know. The anarchism she engaged in with Frankie and Sid and Roz was the same but forever different from the one she had grown up with. Roz felt the same about Jewishness, the Jewishness she engaged with now at the deli with Frankie and Sammy and Sid, it was nothing she could talk about with her father the kosher butcher whose namesake had made her Roz the Kosher Butch, a homage to her father, to her family, how it made her feel closer to them but they'd never know anything about it. Like Frankie's mother's cap maybe. How when she wore it it was in memory of her mother, but how it made her look like something her mother would never even recognize. Despite all the solidarity Sammy felt lonely. She wondered whether if she'd been rejected she would have felt more seen. To accept and to reject something is the same, it's the same amount of understanding only you choose whether to like it or not. But really her mother saw her of course she did, she saw how her hair hung in her eyes and her jeans were blue and her jacket was blue but her mother didn't read butchness like the girls in the bars did. She read butchness through the glasses of the proletariat just like she read everything else. Butch was one uniform of the proletariat and she and her children were that. And of course Asha should have seen Frankie like that, the way he saw everything else. "But being a man is very complicated" he'd said "it is very complicated to be a man."

MEETINGS

[Meeting of the BOP at Louis' Place on "What it Means to be a Movement."] In attendance Louis [convener], Sammy Silver [taking minutes], Sammy, and Harry Harlem. "It's important to have a secret handshake" [SHAKE] "It is!" "People should have a handshake which says *I see you*" "Yeah!" "A secret handshake is of high importance" "Write that down" [writes] "And it's important to have a code name" "A code name" "Like Greenbay" "Or Soul Fox" "Dreambuster" "Or Tree Top" "Or Miss Me" "Or Jelly Pop" "Or Spring Clean" "Write these down" [writes] "And it's important to have a paper circulating" "A publication" "A pamphlet" "Something in print" [write that down] "Which people can read over their cereal in the morning" "On the train" "Over coffee" "Can pass around" [writes this all down] "Can contribute to" "Pass comment on" "Get angry about!" "Lend around" "Ball into a ball and chuck" "And about that handshake" "It goes [ring-finger pinky-ring slap hands twice] or [shake fist shake fist ring-finger pinky-ring slap hands shake] or it goes [wave shake pinky shake pinky fist shake]" "Yeah! Try [side slap slap shake] or [shake left] stop! [shake right] stop! [shake left touch left slap left twice] write that down!" "And since it's the—" "BOP!" "—we shake hands like we're playing the piano! Shake hands like?" "Playing the piano! Shake hands like?" "Playing the piano shake" "Hands like playing the piano like?" "Shake hands! Shake" "Like playing the piano like" "Shake hands like playing the piano like?" "Playing the piano shake" "Hands like" "Playing the piano!" "Since it's the BOP!" "Write that down!" "And about that! What's it called?" "The Rag" "The Level" "The Bottom Line" "The Life and Times" "The Rattle" "Yakety Yak" "Don't talk back" "I'll be your paper boy" Sammy said. They assigned roles: in the role of paper boy Sammy [spotlight on Sammy who gives the audience a wink and tosses rolled up papers from the stage into the audience *toss* and *toss* and *toss* and the audience goes wild scrabbling to have one of those papers to hold and waving it over their heads saying "I got one I got one! Oh I got one I got one!"] In the role of printer: Sammy Silver [spotlight on Sammy Silver and the audience is silent, rapt as she mimes perfectly the actions of using a mimeograph: loads the invisible paper, turns the invisible handle, loads the invisible paper, turns the invisible handle. The audience's mouths gape like watching an ice skater or a tightrope walker. The invisible papers float through air, rocking side to side then landing and Sammy comes to the front of the stage and stands among them and takes a bow.] In the role of editor: Louis [a big cheer goes up! "The editor! The editor!" The spotlight is a warm circle around her, Louis! That face behind the bar, it's Louis! She goes coyly up to the stage, shading her eyes from the lights. She's not used to it, takes a shy little bow and the girls go wild. Louis the editor! Cheer cheer! Louis lit up there, no one had seen her legs before just her arms and shoulders her sleeves rolled up to the middle of her biceps which reached to grab bottles and poured and now they saw the waiter's apron round her waist like a tool belt, rags to wipe down the drips. Cigarettes. A bottle opener on a chain.] In the role of journalist: Harry Harlem ["Ladies and Gentlemen our man out in the field" and Harry's lit up, a long line from one shoulder to the other, from the top of her head to her toes. "What does it mean to be a movement?" Harry licks her lips in the light and the crowd lick their lips right back.] In her role as paperboy Sammy would go scooting round the bars saying *Hot off the press it's The Note kids. It's the latest Note read all about it read all about it* dropping off stacks to the coffee shops and Sammy Silver'd take them to the deli, all the spaces that are just the same but smell different. And Louis reports back that "The people are using The Note as a coaster" and Sammy says "They're scribbling down phone numbers on it." They're shredding it waiting for dates to arrive, nervous at the bar, nursing a coke and it's going flat and they're shredding it, biting at their bottom lips, shaking their knees, coke's going flat the whole time and a pile of shredded paper curls at the foot of their barstool. She's not there yet. She's late. Is she? But she turns up. "Sorry to keep you waiting" "I'd wait" Sammy smiles. It's the first time they've met not on a Friday. Lily is a wet stroke of paint. Sammy is a block of wood. Lily is a wet stroke of paint. Sammy is a block of wood. "The weather's no good" Lily says, sitting on the barstool next to her new Sammy and getting the bartender's attention, ordering a drink. The jukebox is playing *you don't own me* and Lily's changing all the *don'ts* to *dos*. She had always harbored an anarchist guilt of wanting to be owned. "I don't know what it is!" she says, they're still at the bar and Lily's long as the barstool her legs out in the aisle leaning back against the bar edge getting her elbows sticky and Sammy's a little embarrassed by how she speaks about everything without worrying who's listening. Lily smiles at her "What about you?" "I'm scared somebody's listening that's all" so Sammy doesn't speak much "I'm scared they're not" Lily says, then "You know, you're a fabulous singer" "Thank you" "I've got a soft spot for them" Lily sighs and orders another drink "And on a Friday I always think you're singing just for me." On Fridays Sammy sat behind the piano and played and sang at the same time, just like a jukebox. The thing was, Lily couldn't separate out the Sammys. Somehow Sammy (Sammy Silver) had formed in her mind as the "original" Sammy and this Sammy the Sammy she was with now her Friday night Sammy seemed always to have to fight for space in her head. She'd think of Sammy: picture it—Friday night at Louis' place, Sammy's there on stage, solid, singing and playing in a single movement then— who's this? Sammy Silver'd sneak in sitting suddenly on Sammy's piano stool right next to her, shuffling closer, their arms tangling up. It was as if the drawer in Lily's mind which filed the S-es was full and Sammy was jammed against all the other Sammy experiences Lily had already had and this fresh Sammy became a kind of rearranged version of the old one. So it was that when Lily was with Sammy there was always an out of joint, off-kilter type of feeling and Lily loved to feel like that. Her magic-eye Sammy. Her funhouse Sammy. Sammy the sublime.

[A Friday Night in the Past: Frankie asks Lily to the Yom Kippur Ball] "Are you um" Shift shift. Wriggle wriggle. "Spit it out Frankie I'm cold can't we go in?" Lily hopping from one foot to the other "I was just gonna ask if you were going to the um" wriggle. Outside her front door on the street in the cold, back from a meeting announcing the details of this year's Yom Kippur ball. Lily pushes her shoulder "Of course I'll go with you to the ball Frankie Gold." Say each other's names. Strings. Violins. Swelling. Suddenly can't feel the cold. Etc etc. Lily inside and still standing on the step heart breathing like a lung. Frankie tap tap tap down the street now, swinging round the lampposts how moments can barge into one another and cause a ridge. Like when tectonic plates hit together and forge landscapes that make weather that give shape to people's lives etc. Rush rush! Inside the hall people danced and ate food with special fervor against god. "I've never seen a bunch of heathens look so much like a bunch of Jews in my life" Lily'd said leaning against the wall outside. It was inescapable the Jewishness, the Jewishness of atheists, of militant atheist anarchists who held balls on the day of atonement "I mean they couldn't bring themselves to serve bacon and eggs could they?" Lily was a teenager and hated her parents who had never done anything but be anarchists and made her go to anarchist school and read anarchist stories. Sammy and Frankie and Lily and the other kids who went home to separate houses but really, fine yes, really they were more like brothers, like comrades, not family but attached, like pairs of socks are attached. They played "Kropotkin" at kids' parties going round in a circle, first putting one grape in your mouth, "Say: Kropotkin" then another, "Kropotkin" and another "Kropotkin" until you couldn't fit anymore grapes in and the winner had a mouthful of sweet grapes and still said "Kropotkin!" they fell about laughing, smushing the grapes in their mouth finally, chewing on the skins. Lily fought with her brother "Are you sulking again Lil?" "Fuck you" he held his heart "Oh no are you going to tell Frankie on me?" "You're disgusting" "Come on sis" "Anarchists don't believe in family, comrade" she said. Fucking brothers everybody was her fucking brother her fucking mother was her fucking brother her fucking grandfather every man at every meeting was her fucking brother them, them them them—she stopped next up was Frankie and when she thought of her, when she saw her when Frankie was there everything slowed down and didn't fling itself about but hung like ears hang from a spaniel. In the summer Frankie wore t shirts that hung off her and shorts which showed her knees. Lily imagined that if her and Frankie ever went anywhere she'd tie the corners of Frankie together and carry everything inside of her like a bindle, that she could use as a pillow, that she could use as a towel, that she could use as a hat. Lily wanted everything of Frankie. Outside the hall she leaned against the wall. People came in and out and music escaped in gasps. Frankie jumps up on Sammy's back and holds her arms out making herself big, and Sammy teeters about beneath her holding her up they're laughing "God will smite you down" she says in her deep voice she's trying to impress Lily but she doesn't know how to be impressive yet. Below her Sammy thinks about it too, the way the keys go down when you press them. "I always thought if I just played piano I'd never have to actually speak to girls I could just play and they'd know all about me" Sammy'd say to Lily years later. "You're good at talking to girls Sam, you always have been" sweet old Sammy. "I'm better at the piano" she'd say still unable to look Lily in the eyes without some kind of regret she couldn't put her finger on and if she couldn't put her finger on it then was it there did it matter? "Don't compare yourself to Frankie" "I'm not" "Frankie's not good at talking to girls she's just good at talking" Frankie was. "Frankie's no good at not talking that's her problem" "How about when she's singing?" "Oh couldn't she have played the piano?" leans in "or better couldn't somebody have handed her a saxophone?" Sammy smiled, leaned back in her chair and played with the spoon in her coffee mug—ting—clink—"I like it when Frankie speaks, Lil" she said gently "but I guess we wanted her to say different kinds of things." Back outside the Yom Kippur Ball they're still kids, and

Frankie short of knowing what it is she should do, tries everything. Frankie is the all-singing all-dancing I'd rather go blind boy she's got [   ] she's got [ ] who could ask for anything more? She's got the sun in the morning she's got the moon at night any song you can sing Frankie can sing better she is a Frankie song book, a Frankie medley, Frankie is auditioning for the part of [   ] who could ask for anything more? "Just come inside and dance with us Lil, it's no fun out here" Frankie hops down off Sammy's back, leans on the wall beside her but Lily's not budging. "It's dangerous you know" "What is" "This ball" "Oh yeah?" "Yeah, you know how powerful the people who go to these synagogues are? You know how hard they're trying to harness the power of god and shoot it out their eyes at us? We took god out of religion, that's alienation, you know that? We're aliens, we're dangerous. You can get into a lot of trouble for being at this ball and I like trouble, all those people in there they all like trouble and I like you Lil" Frankie said "so I reckon you must be trouble too."

"You know what punk means Vic?" Vic is wearing a leather jacket. Under her t shirt her undershirt is white too. Vic washed her t shirts and her undershirts with her pharmacist's coat. "The last thing you hear before somebody bops you in the side of the head?" "Nah"

Laur sucks on cigarette "punk is bread, and *some boys* is punk too" smoke "that's prison talk men's prison, of course you know who the punks are in prison don't you? some boys, yeah, some boys like us" flick cigarette, done with it. "You ever been out to that bar where Marg goes?" "Yeah" "I never went." They're on a bench in the park. It's green out. "You know those ads on milk for lost people?" "Yeah" "It puts you off your milk" Laur sparks up another cigarette, her leg is going up and down up and down "who do you call to get your son's face on the milk anyway? The milkman?" "No" Vic says "Well who?" Laur says "I dunno do I?" "You know those plastic blowers they use to set hair?" "You ever stop talking?" "You ever start? You know I think when those blowers are down over your head they eat your brains out HEY Vic! You get your hair set recently? You missing something? Your head empty?" Laur's got her palm up like she's gonna slap Vic around the ear. Vic shrugs. It's disappointing, the whole thing, the whole day, it's disappointing. "Jesus Vic you called me remember?" "You gave me your number" "Oh ok wanna go back further? Who invented the telephone wanna start there?" "Yeah well you *gotta* talk on the phone!" Vic says "when you're sitting together in the park you don't." Vic *had* called Laur "Hello?" "Hello? Vic?" "Yeah" and they'd ended up talking about music, or was it that they'd ended up singing? [Vic is on the phone, which

78

is attached to the wall of her apartment, she has an old barstool by it, tall enough to sit and talk, and she's sitting on it now] "Well hey slick, you caught me, I'm not normally home you know, or wherever I am" Laur means because she doesn't have a home necessarily but a few places she stays with friends, moves around. "You going out?" "No you?" "No" "What's playing?" "Oh can you hear that it's Sur she's playing records" [Laur's staying at Big Sur's using Big Sur's phone] "Does she mind you using the phone?" "No she doesn't mind, what is it Vic did you call to say hello or goodbye? Which is it?" "Hello, hello, that's all" "Ok great, so stop trying to get out of it will you?" "What's she listening to?" "Pop music" "I like country music" Laur smiled but made sure Vic couldn't hear it. "Yeah what do you like about it?" "The pictures" "They don't play it much in the bars" "Psst" Vic made a sound like that "they only play music to get close to girls to" "I like that type of music" Laur was bouncing walking about the apartment whilst everybody else was there, Big Sur playing pop music and Big Sur's girlfriend and a couple of people who hung around, walking until the chord tugged and she had to walk back. "It's fine" "No country music though is it?" "No" quiet for a while, then Vic says "The whole country's in that music" "New York?" "Yeah, sometimes" "I thought they called it country music because it was about Texas" "They call it country music because it's about America" "You like America Vic?" Vic shrugs and Laur can hear it. Anyway it wasn't that Laur wanted Vic to speak it didn't matter if she said anything to her ever again she knew what she was thinking, they were both choking on the same thing so why didn't she just spit it out? It was frustrating that's what it was, that's why Laur kept babbling on, on the bench, about punks and boys like them, about lost boys on milk cartons because it was frustrating to be choking on the same thing, to know the feel of it in your throat and remember how it tasted, metallic and green, not like the park was green more like an alien green that's how it tasted. No Laur wouldn't have minded sitting in silence over the phone, feeling the receiver pulse in her hand until she was hungry enough to chew through the cable the texture of pork fat and follow it until she was on the other end of the line. "Well, yeah but I don't know why, 'cause I don't think America likes me." And Vic holding the receiver, feeling it flutter in her hand like a bird. The thrum of its little heart. Talking about music. Or are they singing. Laur said "You can't like everybody. It's about staying out of people's way" "Oh yeah, where dyu learn that scrappy?" Laur smiled and Vic could hear it "I learned it I just didn't get enough practice at it yet" "You've had more fat lips than, than anything!" Laur was laughing and Vic could hear it. "I stay outta people's way they just get in mine"

"Oh yeah and where you going anyway that nobody can interrupt?" "Nowhere" they say, together. Laur had gone to church as a kid, she thought god was probably watching, she wondered why he never got in her way. Frankie would have said that god was in her way, my rod and my staff they comfort me, thou preparest a table before me in the presence of my enemies thou anointeth my head with oil, my cup runneth over, that means spills, her mother had said, it means it's so full it starts to overflow, that's what it means. Yeah, Laur'd thought, maybe. But that's not how she'd experienced spilling since she'd left her mother or whatever way it'd happened. Spilled blood, spilled beer, but nothing spilling because it was too much, too much to fit, the way she'd experienced it her cup barely had anything in it at all, and still it spilled. Still Laur thought she heard choruses of angels, at her very best, looking her most polished, wearing her whitest t shirt and her bluest jeans she felt like she was leading a procession of angels, her rod and her staff, her hair slicked back, that's how it felt in the mirror, combing grease through her hair, a holy feeling, thou anointeth my head with oil. I shall not want. That was the part she could never puzzle through. I shall not want. Shall I ever. Still maybe that's what Vic could hear too, when she saw her, maybe that's what Vic didn't want to speak over when she asked to meet her. Just to sit in the park and hear what it was she thought she could hear in the presence of Laur, a chorus of angels which promised her someday, someday she'd be rid of all this want.

Surly's name was Shirley but Surly was butch and so was she so she went by Surly instead, which is a name she'd stolen from the boys at school who'd called her Surly Shirley. Then in the bars "Romi, this is Surly" and she'd put out her hand "Call me Sur" known around the bars as: Big Sur. "Why do they call you Big Sur?" "Cause I'm a trip" she'd say and the girls would roll their eyes. Truly Sur was from California, "There's bears there too" "Oh yeah?" "Yeah but the scary kind, not these puffed-up cobs of corn. I grew up in the mountains, it's just rugged rock up there, not pastures and trails, not like you can just go out there and wander, it's tough up there, sure you can drive to the beach, where it's easy but if you turn around you'll see the mountains looking back at you you know how that feels?" With girls in bars she talked about California like she was a holiday they could take, come with me, I'll take you there. It's late one Friday night after a sold-out per-formance from Frankie Gold and Sammy Silver, and Frankie's at the bar with Big Sur. They're talking together and when Joanne's not serving she's hanging around where they're sitting, polishing glasses. Sur's a bit older, it took her longer to get to New York, "It's a long way to California" she said. She was always pleased to bump into Frankie, she saw her sing a lot of course, but every now and again they'd end up at the bar together and it'd be a good time, Frankie was a good talker and Sur wanted that sometimes. Her father had been a talker, they really were mountain people—"although it's complicated, to call yourself mountain people, when you're from where I'm from, because you can always go swim in the sea if you want to, in the same day, in the same hour if you want, I always had that, real high and real low both together, I think about that"—her dad had taken her out walking through the mountains. Sur knew about puff from a young age "Just stand up as big as them if you see them, yeah like that" Sur making her shoulders wide and her chest big and her father saying "yeah, that's it, that's it" pulling her shoulder up even higher, standing on tiptoes, making herself as big and as wide as a bear and her father praising her for it "that's it, and look them in the eyes" her father pretending to be a bear and looking her straight in the eyes "that's it, don't run if you see them ok? Just face them remember?" yeah, she fucking remembered. "I think you're right, Sur" Frankie said "I think we can call ourselves *mountain men* or *city people* you know" Frankie made little actions for the type of person she was being "we're not impermeable to the conditions

83

we grow in, that's what you're saying" maybe it was. "I went fishing as a kid" "That's the most American thing I've ever heard Big S" Frankie pinched Surly's shoulder and shook her head "I'm telling you, you Californians, it's like" shaking her head "they call me Gold!" throwing her hands up. "I'm city people now though" "Psst, comparatively maybe, yeah, maybe but really Sur, and I don't mean to hurt your feelings, you still look as though I should toast you on the fire" they laughed, got a beer. "Where dyu grow up Joanne?" "Just about where you're sittin boys" they both looked about, trying to imagine a child in the bar. They looked and they looked but the only way they could imagine it was if the kid turned up with their hair greased back. It was like trying to imagine planting seeds in the bar. Sur imagined it, scattering seeds on the dance floor, how they'd get ground to dust before they even sprouted and *pah* would they ever? If the dance floor ever saw light it wouldn't be able to believe its eyes, if light ever got in here the dancefloor would burst open, probably it'd grow grape vines from the spilled wine or potatoes from the vodka, or butch fields of rye. Up, up suddenly like a fist through a pane of glass. But maybe Frankie could imagine a kid in a little room with people all packed inside it, a kid sure but not like the type of kid that becomes anything else, a kid who's a kid their whole life. "It's no California" said Joanne "It's *Valhalla*"

Frankie said, really believing it, believing it a great hall where great people came "really Joanne, you grew up in a great togetherness, we're similar like that, both of us, we grew up among meeting, don't you think that's something?" "Better than parting" "I'll drink to that" clink "Exactly, exactly better than parting, a great togetherness, really, and you did too Surly" getting going "when I imagine the land there, how you talk about it, that's what it is isn't it? the mountains by the ocean, a great togetherness there too, a grand meeting, everything from a grain of sand to a hunk of rock" "That's me of course" Sur smirking "Yeah until you zoom out on it, then you're just a grain a' sand again. No really, really I don't mean to get biblical" swilling her mouth with beer "I can't stand to, but the books, of course my father would kill me for saying it, the books aren't all bad I think, I think really all the writing I grew up around, because you know I grew up around it, if not writing then speaking at least, but it's something to do with the masses—" Frankie stopped, remembering then where she was and feeling as if she'd just drawn a hammer and sickle from her bag and had started waving them around. *Masses* she'd said, only she'd felt as if she'd said *Marx* stumbling over "m" words and "c" words in case people saw her looking like a Jew and heard the "cuh" sound coming out of her mouth and didn't wait to see she was only going to say "cough syrup"

85

not "communism" only going to say "coffee" or "coca cola" or "corporation" "condemnation" "colosseum" "cauliflower" for god's sake "collapse" "contraption" "contradiction" fucking "consumption" "condescension" was only going to say "completely" totally and utterly only going to say "clowns" "class" no can't say that say farce sure say pass, please god, say pass, oh and definitely crass, don't pay me much attention, I'm just saying coca cola, just coffee, only company, compatriot, only carefree, only care less. "California might as well mean the moon anyway" Sur said, turning to go "feels that far away. Unbelievable too." She put on her jacket and looked good. "Great to see you Frank" slap on the back "See you round Surl" "See you round."

[Meeting of BOP at Louis' Place. In Attendance: Louis, ~~Harry Harlem~~, Sammy, Lillian] ("Harry's the only one with a membership card so Harry's always off the record, too much hassle" Sammy explained.) "Lily this is Louis" "Hello Louis" "Hello Lily" "You're a friend of Sammy's?" "You could say that" "Sammy said you grew up togeth—" "Oh *Sammy* Sammy, yes I'm a friend of Sammy's" Sammy shifted in her seat "But she's a *friend* of Sammy's" Harry says "Shut it Harry" says Sammy. "Silver not coming tonight?" "Not tonight" "Well then sorry sweetie, it's not a great turn out" says Louis and Lily tells her "Well my father always said two's a meeting" "I count four!" "Well that's two meetings" Harry groans "*Two*? can we make the first one quick?" "You got somewhere to be Harlem?" Lily was used to much bigger union meetings of course. Hundreds of women most times yelling too like a family dinner but this was more like being in a bar. Around the little table everybody smoked. ("Louis's gonna take the minutes" Sammy explained.) Louis had a pencil behind her ear and a ledger folded open on the table, an ashtray on one side holding it flat. Louis smoked and wrote with the same left hand so when she wrote she rested the cigarette between her lips and when she smoked she put the pencil behind her ear. The pencil pushed the top of her ear forward and Lily thought it made her look like a little boy. But Louis had a hold on everything. Her ear held the pencil and her lips held the cigarette which filled the ashtray which held the ledger in place. "All right all right we've all got places to be" "Bigger stages" "Yeah Louis, write that down" "And bigger pay packets" "Yeah, yeah Louis" Sammy pointed at the ledger "Get that, get that down" "Any song requests in this week?" Louis rested the cigarette on the edge of the ashtray and licked her fingers and flicked through the ledger to a page headed Requests. "Just club stuff" Louis told them "Frank Sinatra Learnin the Blues" psst, get with it "La Bamba, Cry

Me a River, Ain't That a Shame, Shake" "Shake" "Rattle" "Rattle" "Roll" "Anything by me?" "Sorry Harry" ("Harry's been composing" Sammy explained.) "I'll put a request in for it Harry" Lily says. "That's sweet of you Lily" "Any other requests?" "I Wanna Be Loved By You." Harry pours them all a drink. "Upstate the division is asking to go in on the paper to pool printing costs, all those in favor show your hands" Harry puts her hand up so does Sammy and Louis puts her cigarette between her lips and puts her hand up then takes her cigarette out her mouth and says "Motion passed" puts it back between her lips to reach for her pencil and writes it down and puts the pencil back, she doesn't drink. She doesn't have enough hands. "Ok next, a couple of the bars still won't budge on the gig share" Harry flicks her cap on the tableside and it makes a crack "Hold off" she says, cracks the hat "Hold off?" "Hold off!" "Sure" Sammy says and Louis writes it down. ("We're holding off on the job share" Sammy explains to Lily though Lily's right there) "Well I'm rooting for you" she says. "Do you sing Lily?" "Haven't yet" Lily was an anarchist. She *still* was. I still am, Lily said, when she woke up each morning and brushed her teeth and looked in the little mirror. Yes, she splashed her face with cold water and brushed her hair out of her eyes and said, I still am. They'd talked about it. About how one day it might go, leave their bodies like a cat who was getting fed better by the neighbors. When anarchism left her body Lily thought—gah!—it was too late! it would be the day she died now. Maybe she'd be hit by a bus and she'd lay on the road and watch her soul leave her body dressed in black and red. She went to meetings like an alcoholic did. She'd only been intending to meet Sammy but Sammy'd had the meeting so she'd met her there. She thought of Frankie. "I can't bear the thought of you meeting somebody" Frankie'd told her. And some other time: "Life's just a series of meetings Lil, union meetings, meetings at the bar . . ." They'd argued. "Oh please" Lily said "does anyone know what Marx's wife was called?" "Jenny" "Apart from you? and you only know because you're interested, you like wives, you love wives, you love them so much you want one!" "I don't want you to be my wife Lil, I'm an anarchist, I want you to, to—" "To be your wife and how many times can you tell me you're an anarchist Frankie Gold? and each time you tell me" she was really going for it now "am I meant to have forgotten in that time?" "What the fuck Lily" "It's just that I've been here the whole time haven't I? I've sat next to you at all the meetings and posted all the posters and marched in all the marches I was there remember? I'm a fucking anarchist too" "Well be glad you're not a Marxist Lillian, Marx had a wife called *Jenny* and they called their first child *Jenny* what type of vision is that? and what type of *homage* is that? to a woman? to have the same fucking name as your father's wife it's fucking oedipal it's fucking disgusting" "If you hate women so much then get the fuck out of here" pointing to the door arm out straight slash slash across her body across the room "I don't hate women Lil, I hate myself that's all" "Oh, well then I can't yell at you anymore then if you hate yourself, I can't be seething just to look at you" "I'm sorry you don't like the bars I can't help that you don't!" arms open and out heavy weighing hands what do you want from me hands and the whole time Lily flipped about, like a flag in the wind, turning away and turning back and waving her arms and her hair moved. *Pah* Frankie thought she's a real patriot now flapping about like a flag, waving and waving like a flag that's what Frankie thought pah pah. Well if she's so American why didn't she like the bars? What kind of American didn't like the bars there were bars for everybody. Irish bars Italian bars gay bars anarchist bars bars for old men bars for young men bars where girls danced on the tables what kind of bar did she want? "What bars would you rather be in any way!" Frankie threw her hands up like her father "you wanna be in the bars with a bunch of anarchists your whole life?" "Oh you'll only gather them to you wherever you go anyway! Of course you will! You can't help it you think you're some butch in a bar but you're not Frankie Gold you're just your dad when he was a boy when he was some heartbreaker like you" *Pah!* Now Lily pah pahed. She'd stumbled in her tirade into reminding herself how Frankie was beautiful like a bed that's been slept in. A boy's bed, in a boy's room. She stopped. Frankie sat on the arm of the chair with her chin on her chest, tugging a loose thread on the seam of her jeans "I don't think anyone's ever called Asha a heartbreaker before" *Pah* they thought together. "Well neither is his kid" Lily said, but it was all calm now. "Sammy is baking cakes tonight at her mother's house" "Why is Sammy baking cakes tonight?" "Big fundraiser tomorrow" Lily nodded. "Sammy said we'd be welcome to come and try a slice" "Is that what you were aiming on doing tonight?" shrug "Sure" Frankie said "a cup of coffee with Sammy and Sammy's mother and some cake? Sure, sure, yeah, yeah I hoped I'd be there doing that tonight" Frankie nodded as she spoke. "Did your mother ever bake?" Lily asked "Nope" "Didn't she have the time?" said Lily "Hardly any" Frankie said. Outside Sammy's door Frankie straightened her jacket and pushed her hair back to make sure it was neat, and Lily stood up her tallest and put on a smile. "Rosa, hi" "Frankie, come in, Lilian" Sammy's mother took both of their hands and squeezed them in her own. "Comrades" Sammy said as they came into the kitchen. "Hey ma how about calling the cake stall Bread and Rosa's?" "How about

Bread and Rosa and Sammy's? You baked them" Sammy's mother spoke to Sammy, to all the children like they were the most sweet the most important creatures on earth. They cut into a cake just out of the oven and it sank like a sigh in the middle and the heat was a part of the taste. To Sammy's mother anarchist children fueled her faith. All the children had grown up together, all her comrades had kids and they'd raised them together, like a, like a litter and now here they were, belonging to nobody but themselves but still her child and Asha's child and Daniel's child and Daniel's child Lily looked so glamorous, so American and Sammy and Frankie looked so much like Rosa had looked as a kid, her and her brothers and sisters, unscrubbed, a kind of ruddiness to them that the world settled onto you and yes Lily looked like that too, really, warm circles under her eyes the color of wine and a little chap on her lips under her chapstick. In her memory Rosa and her brothers and sisters wore one big shirt, a shirt just big enough for all of them to stand in, in a row of five each of their heads poking out of the collar, all of them squirming under it to be the person whose arms fit through the arm holes. Rosa's father had worked in a shoe factory "And if I didn't" he'd exclaim, "you wouldn't have any shoes!" Rosa repeated it now round the table: "Your grandfather worked in the shoe factory of course" "I know" "Yes, and he used to say—" "—He used to say" Sammy does an impression of her grandfather: "And if I didn't! You wouldn't have any shoes!" This was how he'd explained the strikes to his children why they were so hungry and angry and always on the streets and Sammy remembered him explaining it to his grandchildren too. "Exactly!" Rosa said "Exactly, and what did he mean by that?" "He meant that the worker makes the shoes" "And if they didn't?" "And, if they didn't, then nobody, not the worker's children nor the owner of the factory himself would have one shoe between them. He meant that without the worker the boss would walk barefoot" "Exactly, and?" "And he meant that without working in the shoe factory he'd wouldn't have a cent to buy shoes with" "So he worked in the shoe factory" "So he worked in the shoe factory!" Rosa held up her arms as if to say so there you have it. Frankie said "If he was an anarchist wouldn't he have imagined making his own shoes for his own feet?" "Of course that's what he was imagining but what about everybody else's feet? what kind of anarchist imagines making himself a pair of shoes without making a pair of shoes for each and every person?" "And how do you do that?" "You do it in a factory" "With a boss" "No not with a boss and you know damn well not with a boss" Sammy balled her fists and talked back at Frankie and Frankie laughed, she knew not with a boss, not with a boss of course not with a boss. She was testing her friend Sam, even though they were the same age, even though they were at Sammy's mother's house sitting with Sammy's mother, even though they looked like daughters in the kitchen, though maybe not like Lilian looked like a daughter. And maybe in some kind of way Rosa found it strange to see her daughter being so much like a man but only when she saw her daughter through a man's eyes, when she looked at Sammy through her own eyes she saw her in fact as almost identical to herself. Rosa didn't think it strange for a woman to be like a man, only men find that strange. Rosa knew it was not absurd for a woman to see a woman thinking, to see a woman teasing, to see a woman laughing, it is only absurd for a man. "Francesca stop baiting my daughter and tell me how is Asha?" "Asha is still an anarchist Rosa" and Rosa rolled her eyes and turned her attention "Lillian, how's your father?" "Didn't you see him Friday?" "Yes I saw him and he was talking about you" "Was he?" "Yes and about your brother" "What about me and my brother?" Lily was still a little sour from her argument with Frankie "That your brother is moving to Pittsburgh." "I'll miss my brother when he goes to Pittsburgh" Lily said, a piece of cake on the end of her fork then in her mouth. The light hits her, and a tune starts "Of course you will" Rosa said "Somehow we miss men more when they go away" wistful sigh, the tune playing "I think we miss them less" "Is it because we expect men to die?" "Men to die and women to multiply" "But mothers die" Frankie said "Yes" "But men die, always in the newspapers, men die, and men kill" "Definitely." Lily's fork glinted in the light and everyone faded into shadow "When your mother died I found it easier to imagine my mother dying, is that awful?" shrug "I wanted to empathize with you, and so I imagined what it would feel like for my mother to be dead, and before long it didn't feel that bad, because I could see you were still alive" ("Not much") "I thought you'd die of grief, but you didn't" "Grief is what stops you from dying when someone you love does. That's what it's there for. So you don't die too." These types of conversations were anarchist conversations. Rosa had had them in Yiddish and they had sounded more radical in an uglier language more truthful, now these American voices only made them sound like the intro to a song. "Don't test grief Frankie, it'll kill if it likes" Rosa said. Later Rosa'd say goodnight and go into the back room and Lily'd leave and Frankie'd see her to the door, and they'd kiss in the hallway, her hands around her waist Lily's arms around her neck. Frankie and Sammy sit round the table just the two of them. I got rhythm I got music I got my man [in unison] who could ask for anything more? "Lily's still mad at me" Frankie says.

"Better start tapdancing" Sammy tells her. Dah da dah dah, dah da dah dah, dah da dah dah [in unison] dobedodo-dobedodoo?

There had been a girl called Rebecca who Frankie met in the deli. She'd been sitting by herself at a table and Frankie thought the table would have looked less lonely without her. "Waiting for somebody?" Frankie asked, standing by the seat across from her "Do you have enough coffee?" tilting her head, feeling some-how that she had to be gentler than she normally was, that sometimes she was too large in her actions as if she were always on stage and trying to reach the back of the room. She told herself that here was a single somebody sitting at a table in the quiet deli for whom she didn't need to do any of that. She liked how it felt, it hadn't felt like that in a while, that she was only talking to one person, not a crowd or an audience, yes probably she had got used to an audience. She set her stance accordingly and her voice. She wished she had a tuning fork to strike on the deli table to make sure they were in the same key, starting off on the right note, together. The girl drank the last of her coffee and tilted the mug like Frankie had tilted her head. "What am I saying!" Frankie said, taking the mug from her "there's never enough coffee!" It was something people said to waitresses, or waitresses said to people. "I'm Frankie" Rebecca said her name was Rebecca. Frankie almost said: are you an anarchist Rebecca? but stopped herself. She wished she had flowers to give Rebecca. She wished she could sing her a song. Soon Rebecca was laughing because Frankie was charming and Rebecca had a rusty kind of laugh, gone rusty from use and being left out in all weathers. Yes Rebecca was quiet and happy and Frankie thought that in the new world a quiet and happy person would be a righteous comrade, just as much of a righteous comrade as somebody sad and loud. Not long after that meeting, Frankie introduced Rebecca to everybody and she started coming along to the deli on Fridays. "What do anarchists do with their dead?" Sid looked at Sammy and Sammy looked at Frankie and Frankie looked at Roz and Roz said: "*Say kaddish!*" big laugh! "Why do you ask Reb Samuel?" Rebecca had been thinking about graves, and whether when you came to lay in one it became your property and if it was your property then, well, was it theft? And if you had gone your whole life never owning a part of the earth only to die and have no choice but to take ownership of a plot then wasn't it a waste to go your whole life without it? "Well, we all go somewhere" said Rebecca "Or, we're all put somewhere so where do you put somebody who's got nowhere?" Frankie closed her eyes to smile, as if the sun had just hit her face. Sammy answered

"If our body isn't ours anymore then how can the hole it's put in be ours? It's all nobody's. The hole, the body, it's all nobody's." Roz had called her Reb Samuel first. Roz and Sid had sized her up the first time they saw her, a girl like they'd grown up with, they teased her like teenagers. Yes they had Frankie and Sammy and each other but a nice Jewish girl? it took everything Sid had not to fall in love with her. "This is Rebecca Samuel, she's joining us tonight" Frankie had introduced her to them at the deli, at their usual table one Friday night and Roz held out her hand and said "Reb Samuel" and Rebecca rolled her eyes and took her hand, "Comrade" she said. "This is Roz" [healthy shiny good Jewish family big butch brown eyes aspirations etc] "and Sidney" [greaseball heartbreaker loyal dog Jewish mother (loud) Jewish father (soft) under achiever loyal loving charming] "and you know Sammy" Sammy smiled. "Reb Samuel" Sid called from the other end of the booth "Don't I know you?" "Afraid not" "Didn't I see you in my dreams?" Sid said "More likely at the deli" Rebecca said, holding her stare until Sid squirmed "I would have noticed you" she said, straightening her back and taking out a cigarette. Frankie thought Sid was really pretty impressive with girls, how she went from dopey to sharp in a way that only music could. Eventually Frankie had asked her: "Are you an anarchist Rebecca?" And Rebecca had gone home with her that night. It'd been hot out and Frankie's shirt was rolled up above her elbows and buttoned down another button "You've never asked me about my childhood" "Should I?" "Not if you don't want to know" "We don't need to start from the beginning, it'll make no difference to the sense it makes" "The sense it makes of what?" "Of a life." No, Rebecca had said, she wasn't an anarchist. Her father read some of the papers but only for the literature. And was Frankie planning to kill the president? "Would it be any different to the violence the president has done to you and me?" Frankie asked. "My father would never have you round the house" "What about your mother?" Frankie asked. Rebecca had been there for the summer, it had been a summer of Rebecca, of soft, thin shirts clinging to Frankie's skin, of Rebecca in dresses, of reading in parks and sleeping with all the windows open

That summer Vic and Laur wore t shirts and jeans and sunglasses and the sun caught on their belt buckles and on the grease in their hair and the rings they wore. "I'm not sure if I've been thinking about you or just thinking" "Isn't that a song?" "It feels like a song, like a song gets into your head." Really they were strutting down the street, in their t shirts and jeans like a ray of light cutting through the concrete like

99

stones set in silver glint glint glint. The ease of access that Vic had to painkillers loomed over her like a plot device. Not that she took them but that she could. Vic was a *pharmacist*! Who the hell had let a pharmacist into the bars? Hadn't they asked her when she got to the bar that first time? Asked her her age and her profession? And hadn't she said I'm sixteen and I'm a pharmacist and hadn't they got rid of her then and there, said no, not here. Everybody here needs you too much, they'll rip you apart, the need, the need they'll have for you, it'll tear you apart. Only it had been the opposite. Vic hadn't said a word about what she did for work, the room full of pills she spent her day in just like she hadn't said a word to her father about how she spent her nights. "You're a *pharmacist*?" "Yeah" "Like a doctor?" "No not like a doctor like the guy who gives you your prescription" "Shit" The pavement sent heat up off it and the two bopped down the street like their boot soles would melt. Laur ran her hands through her hair to slick it back "Got brains then V" "You got brains too Laurie" Vic'd been sweet recently, had decided to be, sick of not being sweet to Laur who made her feel sweet. "I haven't got enough money to have brains, or enough time" Laur stopped to light a cigarette "I got not enough of anything to have much" kept walking glint glint. It'd gotten so that they both knew what was going on so, fuck, Vic would rather have Laur with her walking in the summertime than see her at Marg's across the table trying not to smile. Vic's bike jacket was slung over her shoulder going tacky in the sun. The pavement sent up heat and they wriggled in it. "I suppose I'll own it" "Own it?" "When my dad dies" "What's he gonna die of with all that medicine you've got?" They bought ice creams. Vic kept her wallet in her back pocket, the denim faded in a square where the edges rubbed against it. They licked ice creams and walked or maybe they stood still and everything else moved past them, all different sorts of people doing all different sorts of things but nothing so different it interrupted anything else. They licked ice creams and Vic thought what a tiny part of this whole fucking world to be licking, one scoop of an ice cream and just the tip of my tongue. Vic'd zoom out and see herself sometimes, looking so nice among everything else, seeing then how all your differences were just parts of it all that didn't normally go together. That maybe people were looking at you because they recognized you, not because they didn't. "Anyway I got my looks" Laur gave her a winning smile and pushed her hands deep in her pockets and on the streets the pigeons were iridescent and their feet went gummy in the heat. Vic's jacket trickled down her back and Laur lifted up her sunglasses for a moment and couldn't see anything at all.

ANOTHER FRIDAY NIGHT

Round the table in the deli, another Friday night oh it's getting to be repetitive but every week Frankie felt such relief to be with them, to sit together with them, she'd have been fine just closing her eyes and falling asleep only knowing they were there. Sid stacked sugar cubes on the table, slumped down in the booth chewing gum and drinking coffee. "My father called me an individualist. I suppose because he thought I was the only queer in the world. But just because you left the left doesn't mean the left left you, understand?" Sammy starts playing a melody, nothing much just one finger on a couple of keys round and round, and Frankie sings *just because you left the left don't mean the left left you—don't you know that—just because you left the left don't mean the left left you* etc etc round and round "I think I'm an individualist" Roz said "Yeah well try not to be" Sid said being a little Frankie, being Frankie-like in the way she was trying so hard to do but couldn't quite and Frankie seemed to be getting tireder and tireder and Sid thought maybe her trying to live like Frankie was sucking the life out of her. Sid could fall into being suspicious like her mother who didn't say certain words out loud in case something heard who shouldn't "Well I was speaking to Marcy" "Who's Marcy?" "And Marcy says that the [   ] are buying the delicatessen by her house and are going to start selling [   ]" "What?" Sid's father says "I can't hear half a what you're saying dear" "Cause I'm not saying half of it! Can't you listen! Yadda yadda" "Why bother?" "Oh come on Roz don't play games" "Shouldn't I do what I want" "Only if I can" "And me" and somebody at the next table stands up: "And me!" and at the counter "And me!" and somebody just leaving stops at the door and turns back "And me!" and everybody in the next booth says all together: "Us too!" *just because you left the left don't mean the left left you.* "Only I never was the left was I?" "No you were the middle" "Exactly and now I find myself among anarchists who tell me I can do whatever I want to do and being as I am [gleaming] my instinct is to do as I please" "So you want the smallest type of freedom then? Only as much as fills your suit jacket. I thought you were a bigger dreamer than that" [she is, Roz is only teasing, really Roz hates the middle she came from and though she'll probably end up there she'd like to end up there on her own terms and at least regret never having been the liberty bell(es juive) she and her comrades had dreamt up in the bars and here at the deli table every Friday night.] Sid's all wound up, taking Roz's bait "You're a fucking piece of work Butcher, you wanna be free how about you take a hike?" Frankie tells Sid to calm down and Roz is laughing, a shape with lion body and the head of a man, a gaze blank and pitiless as the sun is moving its slow thighs, while all about it reel shadows of the indignant desert birds. The darkness drops again; "But now I know that twenty centuries of stony sleep were vexed to nightmare by a rocking cradle, and what rough beast, its hour come round at last, slouches towards Bethlehem to be born?" "The center cannot hold" "That's what Frankie read out at her bar mitzvah" Roz keeps teasing and Sid laughs [you piece a' work] "I would've!" "Frankie had an anarchist bar mitzvah" Sid teases too "they called her up to the front and she had to read an article from that month's Stimme" keeps teasing and they all laugh "and all her comrades lifted her up on a chair at the after party singing hay hay daloy politsey" haw haw haw. Frankie had never stepped foot in a synagogue and only ever reached the bar. "I am going to make next week's meeting so fucking boring Sidney you'll wish you would've joined the Communist party" "You call this a party?" says Roz and Sid says "What are the girls like over at that Communist party?" and Roz shoves her on the shoulder "You're a creep Stein."

"Where's Rebecca tonight Frankie?" "She's at her mother's for dinner" And they all raised their eyebrows then, like rolling hills and they leaned back in their seats and were silent. Sid stacked sugar cubes and stuck her gum under the table and, after a while, where they all seemed to be dreaming or trying not to think at all Sammy said "Maybe she'll bring us some leftovers." A piano starts up again, just the right hand playing the melody (whilst with their left hands) they pass the gravy boat (whilst with their left hands) they rub their bellies.

Elsewhere the All-Americans are drinking bottles of beer and eating peanuts. It made Vic want to puke how many people had touched those peanuts. Vic wore a pharmacist's coat all day bright white then at night she put on all black apart from her t shirt of course which was bright white like her pharmacist's coat but her leather jacket was black and her hair was black under the grease and her jeans were black and her shiny shoes were black and her motorbike was black. Was it that she put on a leather jacket and became a butch? Or was it that she took off a leather jacket and became a pharmacist? Or was it that she put on her pharmacist's coat and became a pharmacist and took off her pharmacist's coat and became a butch? Whatever it was Vic felt like a fraud. Like

she could keep peeling off coat after coat and she'd
never get to anything but more coats. Vic lit a cigarette. Marg is saying: "Bartender's on the bar yelling
I'm gonna fucking kill you all if you don't kill each
other first and there are sirens outside and" and Laur
remembered everyone had blurred into one another,
that the bar had looked like a giant leather jacket
flung onto the floor like somewhere there was a butch
bigger than any butch had ever dreamed they could
be who'd arrived and flung off her jacket—"and the
jukebox is playing where the boys are [Marg sings it
moves her arms like a conductor] you know: wheerrree
the booys arrre etc etc and everybody's barging into
one another and holding each other back" Marg is
loving it, retelling the bar brawl, her heart beating
faster, taking big palms of peanuts and Laur remembered how the glass sprayed like a fountain in bottle
green and red. Real blood of the people they usually bought beers with "till he holds me, I'll wait
impatiently" Marg is singing, and flailing her arms
showing how they swung for one another and Laur
remembers how the music swelled and their bodies
started to swell and Vic can't picture it clearly just
sees a giant bardyke flinging her leather jacket on
the floor. "And the bartenders yelling get the fuck
out my bar you barbarians, you bardykes—*where the
boys are, where the boys are*—the song's on" and Laur
remembers all the other sounds glug glug and thud

and someone's laughing. Vic remembers turning to see Laur laughing—glass like a fountain—and how she stopped to watch her and around her arms are swiping like they're wiping tables the same movements, over and over. Beautiful sprays of glass arch over them and catch the light and scratch their cheeks and Marg is pointing "Here, and here, and here" at the parts of her face and her neck where it caught. And Vic thought maybe we're too old for this, maybe violence is something you grow out of which is sad if it's all you've got. Laur says to Teddy the end of something Vic didn't hear the beginning of and they laugh. Vic goes to the bar and orders another drink. "Hey hunk" Laur says. Vic turns "Hunka' what?" she says back. "You waiting for somebody?" Laur says "Nobody special" "Lucky for you" Laur said "she ain't here if she is." "You're wearing a tie tonight" "Yeah I'm old school you got a problem?" "You look smart" "Yeah and you look dumb" like this was the only thing they could start. Vic walks back to the others. It got later and Laur's tie got looser but the knot got tighter. She kept pulling it one way then the other one way then the other like a dog trying to take off its own collar. "Forgettin-I-got-two-lef-feet" Laur slurs to this girl she's standing too close to, stinking of beer near, and spitting when she speaks but it could just be that she's filling up and spilling over. Trying to dance and stumbling about. "You gonna do something about that?" Teddy sat with Vic in the booth. "Are you?" Teddy sighed and pushed himself up. If Teddy was a piggy bank he'd be empty. Butchness had been kind to Teddy, to let him sit in it like a sofa for eternity, knowing there was probably some other seat he should be sitting in. Yeah maybe there were a few coins under the cushions of Teddy but Teddy had been so thoroughly rifled through, so shaken about so turned upside down in this life of his that Teddy wouldn't go searching again. And butchness had never asked Teddy to move along, and it had never fallen through, no it had couched him gently enough and Teddy had left his impression on it, a dip the same shape as him so that yes, butchness had been there but it most definitely wouldn't have been the same without him. "You being a schmuck for a reason greasemonkey" he grabbed Laur by the top of the arm "or you need someone to give you one?" "Don't take a bite out of me Ted I ain't worth chewing" "I know it, now come over here will you, you're dripping all over the dance floor" "Am I raining?" "Yeah" "Can I stay at yours tonight Teddy?" All Laur's stuff was under the table, she'd come to the bar looking smart hoping to hook up with somebody smart, whose bed was smart whose life was smart whose smart life she could fall asleep in. "The bar was churned up" Marg had told them how after the brawl the place had looked "ploughed like a field"

Marg'd said. And Laur slipped about on the dance floor, Teddy holding onto her arm like a new calf. Full to spilling, it had begun to cascade down the sides of her "it smelt like it too" (Marg) "like soil, fields of mud" splashing and gulping. Teddy held her arm. Different from how you held somebody in your arms and swayed but not so different that it didn't look a dance. How she skidded, her legs going wide and splayed and how Teddy pulled her up again like picking a carrot out the earth or pegging washing on a line (it'd never dry) gulps, splashes.

Frankie's home alone writing. A lamp on in the living room and a typewriter on the coffee table and Frankie on the couch with her legs apart making space for her arms typing clack clack fast with a cigarette out her mouth like her father had looked and all the men you ever saw like that, then Sammy comes home. "Why dyu have to smoke when you write? Does writing make you forget you're a singer?" Sammy takes Frankie's cigarette out her mouth and smokes it "It's a part of the atmosphere" Frankie keeps typing "Is it lyrics?" "For what, the charts?" "Or the stage" "Did I miss the memo on people wanting to hear us sing originals?" "We're working on it at the BOP" "The dance sensation that is sweeping the nation" "That's the hop" "Well then let's go to the hop" "Oh baby."

Sammy sits down next to Frankie, starts yawning and closes her eyes and soon she's dreaming. Sammy being there had never interrupted any of Frankie's thinking or writing. She could write a poem when Sammy was there, or come up with a song, or a letter to the editor. Frankie had been published frequently since she'd left her father's house in her father's boss's newspaper only anonymously. Letter to the Editor Regarding Your Use of the Word "Deviant" to Describe the New York Nightlife, Dear editor, is it simply nighttime which is deviant to you? Does the editor believe that American values have something to do with sunlight? And since when did the editor of any anarchist paper have any interest in the propagation of American values anyway? Letter to the Editor Regarding Mutual Aid and the Dissemination of the Family, Dear Mr editor, does it occur to the anarchists that having a blood tie to another human being does not make them more worthy of our responsibility but can sometimes when put into action make them worthy of less? Does it occur to the editor and to his readers that blood ties need to be tended just as much—no more or less—than our other ties, our bonds of brotherhood? Asha did or didn't know it was Frankie. She sent her articles to the music press and sometimes she sent her poems. Mostly they piled up, really, stacks of paper and Sammy read them and said yeah I like it or, didn't you write this one already? By

her Sammy dreamed, twitching her leg like a dreaming dog. She was in the living room of their childhood
the one which in dreams like this was always funnel
shaped, wide at the top and small at the bottom and
she always shuffle shuffled towards the middle hoping
no one would see and just as she was about to slip
down and out of the funnel to where? she'd wake up!
Or something else would happen which would make
leaving impossible. In this dream the living room was
full and Frankie's father was reading poetry from a
pile of poems almost as high as his hip, he'd read one
and reach down and pick up another and another but
the pile never went down. The living room was full,
people standing everybody on all the couches and the
kitchen chairs and she was sitting on the carpet with
the children but with the adults too, who held the
children to them and squeezed them at moments of
exultance, scruffed their hair. Sammy sighed in her
sleep. "Did you hear that? Did you? I hope you're
listening kid, can you feel it?" they'd ask, and she
could, the lasting pinch on her shoulders. Frankie's
father read his poem:

I HAVE WRITTEN FOR YANOVSKY;
a poem by Asha Gold

I have written for Yanovsky,
So you better mind your kopvsky

If you want to
Open doorskys
Sell your soul to
Saul Yanovsky [laugh]

Once I was a wannabe it
Then I let Yanovsky see it

If you want to
Open doorskys
Sell your soul to
Saul Yanovsky

Now I've written for Yanovsky
See the size of new kopsky? [hawhaw]

If you want to
Fit through doorskys
Get a no from
Saul Yanovsky

Once I was a no-good poet
Now I'm a poet and don't you know it!

I have written for Yanovsky!
See the swell of my swell kopvsky?
I can barely fit through doorskys
Opened wide by Saul Yanovsky.
[squeeze, scruff etc]

In the living room, sitting next to Sammy dreaming,
Frankie was writing a play: [Man walks in dressed
very smartly and looks clueless] MAN: You always

seem to need to use the toilet when I'm ready for bed! [Man is speaking to his pet poodle. Man is in the street outside his house]. The play was a staging of a meeting of anarchists in a living room like the ones of her childhood. In this scene the man had just finished tidying up after the meeting and was, as he said, ready to go to bed but the poodle needed to piss so he'd taken the poodle outside and was waiting for the poodle it was, Frankie thought, a way of reversing roles. The whole play the man would be trying to get on with the great business of toppling the government and redistributing the wealth among the people and meanwhile his poodle and all the other pets kept asking for things and pulling their owners in different directions on their walks. Refusing to bring back balls and pissing wherever they wanted were eating on the floor were organizing, really, they were. And Frankie imagined the fleas on the backs of all the dogs and cats and maybe someone had a rat they kept in their top pocket no, a parrot! Yes! Frankie laughed at the revolutionary, the anarchist who kept a parrot who had been his mother's parrot who was older than him, much cleverer than him and who of course sang the Internationale whenever it liked which was getting the man into much trouble with the neighbors "Shut up shut up!" he'd hiss at the parrot whenever it started singing and the parrot would reply: "Traitor." There were no women in the play but Frankie imagined staging it in the bar and all the dykes playing the pets. They never spoke (apart from the parrot) but had long rambling stage directions to follow to do with the looks they gave one another. Their pooling mirror-black eyes looking lovingly at one another, cat and dog, rat and cat. Frankie was doing her best to imagine everybody, all things, but her mind kept bumping up against the walls the world had built in it. She thought zooming in was a decent writing technique for trying to outdo the limits of her mind, to bamboozle herself. To not look out and out and out but in and in and in so everything got bigger and clearer and not smaller and blurrier. A blur, though, that seemed like something she could work with, Frankie scribbled the word blur down and thought she'd work on something maybe a poem about it later. The play of course was a musical and she would be in it, and Sammy would score it. The dykes dressed up as pets would look lovingly at each other on stage and as the animals got smaller the dykes would get bigger, zooming in and in the really big butch ones playing fleas who lifted each other up with no effort above their heads and sat on each other's shoulders FLEA ONE: We're as tall as you like! FLEA TWO: As wide as you need! FLEA CHORUS: We're as tall as you like [two three] We're as big as you need [repeat]. *Me as flea two??* Frankie scribbled down. She was going to ask Roz to play a Doberman called Dewey. She thought next time she ran into Surly she'd see how she felt about playing an American spaniel named Samuel. Yeah Frankie just kept writing whilst Sammy slept by her and dreamed, her head back and her legs sprawled out and her hands resting on her thighs. Sammy was taller than Frankie by a head or so but Sammy was always sitting down and Frankie was always standing and Frankie was always at the front of the stage and Sammy was always at the back. No one had stopped Sammy looking how she looked or living like she liked to but she didn't. Sammy wasn't doing what she wanted or living like she liked, though *she was nearly*. She wore the clothes she wanted and didn't have to change them for work. She played the music she wanted though she wanted to be better, to play the best music, her and Frankie both wanted that, to write and play music that was in some way close to the feeling it gave them when they played it. Sammy had never had to pretend much only to be quiet and to go along no her mother had seen her hair get short like plenty of the women to whom anarchism had meant a complete disregard for what was and wasn't allowed but really Sammy wanted to grow her hair long. Not like a girl does but like a boy does. Sammy wanted first to be a boy and then grow her hair long like a virtuoso, like a beatnik, like some of the boys were doing now. Instead she cut it short not bothering to become a boy with long hair but to exist instead in asymmetry with what she wanted, to be a girl with short hair. She cut it short around the sides and left the front a little longer and she didn't slick it back like the others did so she could have, at least, the same view as the long-haired boys who saw the world through the hair falling over their eyes.

"Good evening Sidney, where is everybody?" "Evening Reb, everybody's late" "For what?" They laughed. "Aren't you with Frankie?" "Apparently" "Oh I see" "Can I get you a cup of coffee Sidney?" "Will it taste any different from the first one?" "Only hotter I'm afraid" "Don't be" Rebecca came back to the table and sat with Sid hunched over pouring sugar into her cup. "My brother is working a high-paying job in another city" she said "And you?" "I feel like I'm sitting with my brother drinking coffee right this minute" "Oh brother" "Oh brother" [sigh and clink clink, tap their spoons on their mugs together and slurp their coffee.] "Slurp" "Slurp" everybody was late. "Does your mother know you're here?" "Does yours?" "With Rebecca Samuel? She could care less" "I suppose so" "Oh brother" "Yeah" [slurp, slurp] "She doesn't know you're an anarchist now though. She isn't so excited by anarchists. Nice Jewish girls, yes, yes, she is excited by them well, not *excited* not like I'm excited by them though I never have been—"

"Never?" "—I've been with nice girls" "Oh?" "And I've been with Jewish girls," but—" and Sid laughed "Oh brother" Rebecca said. "Listen Reb Samuel if my mother comes in here don't show her your union card ok?" "And if my mother comes in here you better hope Frankie's still running late" "Must be a big night at the bar" "Didn't you go?" "I like hearing them play I really do, I love hearing Frankie sing really, I think Frankie singing is the last thing I'd wanna hear on earth, really I do and the way Sammy plays piano really I like it, I do, but lately Frankie's heart's not in it and I can't get to enjoy it if I know she isn't. I'd rather not hear it at all" slurp "didn't you go along?" "I couldn't bear to hear the love songs" "But you're here" "Well is it tonight she was planning on telling me?" "About love?" "Is tonight's meeting on love?" "Would you leave if it was?" "If it was it'd be about loving something you can't hold" "That's pretty, Reb Frankie make you a poet these past few months?" "Is this how poets feel?" That summer'd been hot and Frankie's shirts had panes of sweat through them and dried out by the open windows and Rebecca had worn dresses. Rebecca had made lemonade and Frankie'd said it'd made her sing the best she'd ever sung and that every time she sang now she'd taste lemonade. And Rebecca had woken up at Sammy and Frankie's house most mornings, grease stains on the pillows and piano keys drawn onto the kitchen table. And

Sammy'd touch a note [touch] and Frankie'd hum it [hum] touch, hum, touch, hum like the notes were coming out the table. Then when Sammy touched the wrong key Frankie'd stop and they'd start over, whilst across the table that summer Rebecca ate breakfast. "Anyway" Rebecca said "if my mother comes in here" she points at Sid "tell her you're my brother."

NIGHT SWEATS AND
SHOWTRAIN TO LENINGRAD

SAMMY'S DREAM

SAMMY: This was my dream. [Sammy lays both hands on the table. Everybody's in the bar, early on a Friday night, they are sitting together in the back corner, it is dark and everybody is smoking and drinking bottles of beer and there's a little dish of nuts in the middle they all keep leaning in—hand, hand, hand—and taking a little handful and eating out their cupped hands but rapt, listening to Sammy who says]

SAMMY: This was my dream, in the beginning I dreamt that we were having a celebration of some kind and the room was packed with people, all my family, all my friends everybody mixed together, from the bars from the printers from my days with Frankie as a kid. Lily was there everybody and the room it's spiraling round and round, everybody's arms around everybody in big circles smaller and smaller all inside of one another and in the middle of course, is me. I'm sitting at a grand piano but I'm small can you picture it? Like a sink full of water you've been doing your dishes in and it's frothy and you pull out the plug and it swirls and dance dance spin spin and there I am, at the center at my piano. No big dream right? I'm always at a piano! [Nuts, beer, glug glug, another etc.] But then, just as I'm putting my first finger on the keys SLAM! [Sammy raps two fingers on the table. The nuts jump in the bowl] the lid comes down and it's gone . . . my finger [Sammy shakes her head, close to tears the others too, they shake their heads like a little herd of cows lowing] it's gone.

ROZ: Oh brother [Roz puts her head in her hands] if I'd have had that dream it would have been about my father [groan] coming to chop off my fingers with a butcher's knife.

SAMMY: [Sammy holds her hand up in front of her, her palm open and her fingers spread. Caught in the light it casts shadows in slats across the bar. She pushes her chair back and stands up, the sweet trembling of music starts, the table turns into the top of a grand piano and still the others are there, gathered around it, Sid and Frankie and Roz and some others, extras who look like them, all hanging on the trembling notes and Sammy says or is she singing] I felt so sorry for my finger [hot tears of grief in her eyes] I thought maybe I should bury it. I wondered who I should invite [the music swells and Sammy says in a singing voice:] The femmes came. Just me, lugging a coffin out to the cemetery and a bunch of femmes dressed in black we got together for this, we reconnected. Gust catches the little coffin, little butch box for the finger tipping in the breeze roll goes the finger in the box. The piano plays and you can hear the sound of fingers on keys but, but, but you can't see them. My fingers are gone and everything I've ever been good at [SID: *no more pressin*] everything I've ever loved [ROZ: *no more pushin*] it falls away because [FRANKIE: *no more playin*] because I can't touch it anymore the way I have needed to [SID: *to touch it*] the way I have needed to touch it [ROZ: *to touch it with my fingers*] the way I have needed to touch it with my fingers. The piano is playing as the coffin is lowered down, playing us out, a tribute to what fingers can do. [The bar starts swaying round the piano, the light diffuses, not a sharp spot on Sammy anymore but a sweet warm light like a sunset over everybody, they sway and they hum and Sammy says in a kind of singing way:] We make small talk at my mother's house, my mother! [SID: *oh brother!*] Everybody helps themselves to the spread, balancing food on napkins in their hands, a gap, where my serviette sags at the space where my finger should be. And Frankie takes me aside and tells me "Don't worry Sam, it'll only make you butcher to have a ring on a finger which stops at the knuckle." And you all sneak me here before it ends. [Sammy looks around. It's a bar now, they're round the table again.] Back at the bar the energy's fading, the way it does, and we put our arms around one another and try to hold it together, we sway and wobble and think of everything we've lost. [The music's lifting out of the room] And Frankie starts singing up on the stage unaccompanied. No piano, just Frankie's voice singing something I don't know, I've never heard it but we love it, really, it's a hit you can feel it [Frankie smiles a thank you] we drink and drink until we're slurring and rubber we've got our arms up or around each other and I thank you all for coming. I'm heartbroken, I say, I'm whistling with loss.

ELEGY FOR MY FINGER

Fuck forever I want you now
that's something you'd say
you were
so overly
romantic.
I lament how I never
put you
in her mouth oh forever
embalmed in the spit of women
who I didn't love
as much as you made them
believe.
Should I stuff you and put you
on my mantelpiece?
Should you stand there

wearing
your own little leather
jacket resewn around you
my finger my lovely finger
how I cried when I held you instead of you
holding me.

I can't get it out of my head, that feeling of looking at where my fingers should be. [They all look down into their palmfuls of peanuts] They're not gone they're just resting in my palm. [Sammy clutches them (fistful of fingers)] I can see it all, all the parts but in the wrong order so my hand doesn't make sense anymore. [Sammy shakes her head] and Sid says

SID: Don't be so sad Sam, it was just a dream. Here, [Sid leans across the table and pulls at Sammy's fingers] they're all attached aren't they? [Pull pull. Sammy smiles and says]

SAMMY: It's only if your hands don't make sense anymore then how do you hold on? I just can't shake the feeling we'll only see each other at funerals, fuck, that this whole thing is just a funeral we're at. Aren't we all here because we lost something? Aren't we here because we've got nothing left to lose?

FRANKIE: What about our chains?

THE END

[Reels of laughter, huge guffaws haw haw and they take a bow laughter rippling out to the whole bar, reeling and rolling laughter retelling itself in different bars and walking home and in write ups it'd all been a set-up to this great joke ha ha ha ha ha ha ha ha haw haw haw haaahahaaa aaaaaHAAA HAHAHA HAW HAHAH HAHAHA!!! HA HA HA HA The whole dream it's a hit. HAHA! The reviews come in: it's a laugh riot a hoot, twist shake rattle rolling in the aisles good one Frankie [Pat on the back Sammy's laughing and nobody can remember what was funny in the first place then they do: *And then Frankie goes: what about our chains!*" Explode! They retell it over and over haw haw haw it carries on it carries on. It always does.]

[Meeting of the BOP at Louis' Place Where After Hours Louis's Brewing Coffee, *aaah*] What everybody has been working on: Sammy was writing a sonata called Night Sweats wanna hear it? [Sammy plays the above.] "Sammy it's good" "Thanks" "It really is. You're unique" "Naw" "You are you are" the two Sammys chat about it. Harry's always writing, the latest thing is called Showtrain to Leningrad. "You like it Silver?" "I love it Harry" "Yeah well" the tune had a kind of shuffling rhythm like you were going somewhere. "Where's it headed?" "Can't seem to finish it" "It's too central, it needs to fall apart that's how it should end" "Fall apart?" "It needs to rattle" [RATTLE] "like a showtrain gone off the rails" "It has" "Well then" "The shuffle's too soft" Louis adds "it's a showtrain isn't it?" "Ok" and Harry plays it harder "Yeah yeah!" they all listen and watch out the window and the showtrain goes and goes. Sammy hops off before Leningrad. There were a couple of notes in Night Sweats that were the same as in Showtrain so if there had been two pianos (which there never were) and Sammy and Harry had played their songs at the same time then *sometimes* the songs would have been the same. You could see it if you placed the scores on top of one another and held them up to the light "See here" the notes are placed the same on the stave every now and again the same way, every now and again, the same words are said at the same time. It showed, Sammy thought, that there was an abundance of people without an abundance of options or it showed, Harry thought, that people shared the same sentiments and used the same tools to express them, the shared tools that we were all able to wield to shape into shape the stuff we had at hand, to play music or to talk talk. "Here" point "that's where the cast first see the snow out the windows, it's the first cold taste of Leningrad and it goes like this" Harry played it and beneath it Sammy's Night Sweats played at the same time, the way Lily saw both Sammys at once.

The same notes in Night Sweats were the serviette sagging in her new hand, it had to do with a gentle pull towards the earth that yes, Sammy supposed you might describe as falling snow. Packing up to go Louis says "See you next week" even though she knows she'll see them sooner. But the BOP meetings were a different kind of seeing, not like seeing in the bar. Harry and Sammy Silver walk out into the night air together, take a deep breath and walk the same way for a while. Sammy tells Harry the reports are in from Leningrad on the staging of Porgy and Bess and the response was cool "Apparently nobody clapped" "They've got taste" Harry said looking cool too, in the night with her shoulders slanting like a slate roof and her cigarette steaming like a chimney pot or— *choo choo*—Showtrain to Leningrad! Harry made a blurred line like a steam train and the sweet blue smoke puffed out of her cigarette "The butcher, the baker, the grocer, the clerk are secretly unhappy men *because* the butcher, the baker, the grocer, the clerk get paid for what they do but no *applause!* They'd gladly bid their dreary jobs *goodbye* for anything theatrical and *why*?" "They've got other business to attend to" Harry said "and I've changed my mind" "Oh yeah?" "Tell Gershwin he can shove it." Sammy and Harry go down different streets now headed in different directions home. "We accidently wrote the same song Harry" Sammy'd said to her earlier over the piano "only they sound completely different!" Sammy's hair flopped in her eyes. She had all her clothes tucked in tightly and her shoes fit well and didn't squeak. She tapped out a rhythm with her fingers pushed into the pockets of her jacket. She kept her head down and walked fast like always and her hair flopped in her eyes. That evening Frankie'd been talking with Sidney at the bar. "People don't just want bread Sid, they want roses" Frankie looked a little dewy-eyed like Sidney's dad's eyes got when Sidney did well. "You mean women?" "No not just women want them, all people, *the People*, the people want roses just as much as they want bread Sid they don't want to just *survive* but to know beauty doing it, what's the point of it? of living without that?" Frankie was drunk, her eyes were watery like she'd cry. Her father'd taught her that, he had, he didn't know whether he'd had the time to, whether she'd been too young to notice any of it but she had understood bread *and* roses too. And she didn't want to die here, with just the bread. "We're the bread is that it?" Sid said to Frankie slumped opposite her elbows sliding on the bar "and they're the roses" Sid chucked her chin towards a group of girls at a booth, different shaped vases of flowers, all kinds of posies like some kind of meadow over there in that booth, of course they were the roses, and they needed Sid, they needed the bread and now Frankie's saying to her that she needs roses, well isn't that perfect?

And Frankie's lolling and sliding and shaking her head, hadn't bothered to wash the paint properly off her face, a smudge of grey across the plains of her jaw left over from the show "We're fucking both Sidney, breadnroses all at once and nobody knows whattado with us" she drooped over on her barstool, put her forehead on the edge of the bartop. Like nobody'd watered her, thought Sid. If she cried now the tears would roll right back into her eyes. Sid put her hand on Frankie's back "But both is what the people *want* Frank, you just said it, and you're the people's favorite act." Frankie grumbled and rolled her head to the side the sticky bar on her cheek the stink of alcohol and coca cola "As we go marching marching" she sang little higher than a whisper "into the beauty of the day" "Come on you bum, you're done for tonight." And Sid hooked her arms around her and stood her on her feet *as we go marching, marching in the beauty of the day a million darkened kitchens a thousand mill lofts grey are touched with all the radiance that a sudden sun discloses for the people hear us singing bread and roses bread and roses.* Frankie thought that singing would summon the revolution. She wondered what song she'd be singing when it finally came. Came like the post came or a chorus came. Would she rush to the streets to this song or that? With all the people, all the people she'd been in this world with in this life all these people would they rush to this? Thick like cream, they'll pour, the people they'll turn into a different substance a creamy pouring substance which will turn the coffee into, into, into something more delicious than that. Ch-chuff ch-chuff showtrain to the outskirts here's Harry blue smoke and all the windows steam with the breath of the people her brain whirred and her heart beat ch-chuff ch-chuff showtrain [SHAKE] bolts coming out of the cars coming apart wave goodbye to your bags to the tracks Frankie's holding herself up on the fridge door, staring into the blue light its soft smell like cat's breath leaking into the room. She shuts it. Rings Sidney— "Sidney?" "No not Sidney Sidney's mother who isn't Sidney's secretary who isn't Sidney's answer machine who is Sidney's mother who owns the phone"—"I"— Frankie tries—"*Yeah?*"—"It's Frankie here is Sidney there?" She called Sidney because it was the only number she had. All the other numbers were girls' numbers and she never called them. She knew Sidney couldn't have been home yet but it was the voice on the end of the phone she needed, any voice, sure she'd talk to Sidney's mother why not. She liked hearing Sidney's mother's voice. She wished Sammy was home but instead Sammy was only on her way. She opened the fridge again, stood in front of it and in the darkened kitchen the little open fridge lit her like a spot. She mouthed along to the radio, pushed her hand through her hair and tucked her shirt into her belt. *I want* she mouthed *a girl—to call—my own I wanna—dream lover so I don't have to dream alone.*

LAST CALL

[A Friday Night in the Past: Packing] "The thing is you can't breed anarchists" Frankie and Lily are at Frankie's, Frankie's packing. "You and I" she said "if we had a kid she could grow up to be anything at all, she might feel guilty about it but that's it" "What about us?" "I know, yes I know, yes I thought that. But then I looked about and it is just us isn't it? Everybody else is gone aren't they?" Frankie looked about. Lily looked about. They were alone. And Lily was about to leave too or was it Frankie? "So it's not blood then" Frankie said "it's bread isn't it?" Every sentence ended as a question because when you asked your voice went up at the end, intoned higher, your voice rose and rose up? and up? and ? and ? and ? ? ? like a segue into a song. But Frankie didn't burst into song [packing pulling shirts off hangers] just spoke like she might. "It was always bread Frankie" Lily said, "anarchism was always bread" "Yeah" Frankie looked down at her feet and Lily said "If you don't breed anarchists then where do they come from? Where did we come from?" "It's not for everybody" "What?" "I mean, it is of course, I mean its intention of course is for everybody but it won't force you to take it, it doesn't tell you what to do does it?" "No" "So it's like a meal, you know, laid out and it's on the table and you take a little of this and little of that but if you don't want to eat some of that other bit you don't have to but if you don't I suppose you'll be hungry" "Anarchists are hungry" "That's it of course" Frankie said "it's hunger that breeds anarchism and if we had a baby I'd rather she never felt hungry and was never an anarchist" "But you're not an anarchist because you're hungry you're an anarchist because someone somewhere is hungry isn't that right?" "Are you hungry Lil?" "I'm an anarchist." Lily stood like a sunset in her room. "What about dykes?" Frankie said. Lily shook her head and sighed the way people do. "Aren't you a boy Frankie Gold?" "Aren't you my wife Lil?" always questions. Up and up and up they ended, trying to sing so they wouldn't have to talk anymore. "I mean, what about dykes don't they give birth to dykes isn't that blood?" "Dykes is roses Frankie, and can't we stop talking in questions now? Can't we say it straight for once?" Up, up, voices rising like ski jumps. Frankie was wearing a white shirt tucked in her jeans. It was undone at the collar showing a white t shirt underneath. And under that and under that and under that, you could only believe there'd be more white t shirts, right down to the bone. The top pocket of her shirt was stuffed with stuff like cigarettes and pens and a handkerchief. Like someone had pierced through the t shirts and there wasn't bone actually just the soft stuff she was stuffed with and through the tear above her heart which looked at first like a top pocket, things had started to fall out. What anarchism had never taught Frankie was how to hold things together. The center cannot hold she knew that ardently. She feared it like Sammy feared losing all of her fingers. Lily said "You feed your child anarchism and you hope that when they're older they'll know that that's what gave them life, all the stuff you need to not starve but if they don't then anarchism will just be somebody else's child instead. Spring up out of somewhere else, somewhere down the street from you or across the road you know, you know what I mean. It isn't your dad's anarchism, it's yours that's what I mean" "I think it's yours" Frankie said "I think my anarchism's just your anarchism isn't it? Aren't I an anarchist because you are?" "You're an anarchist for the same reasons I am, because we were born into it and we liked it, we were fed on it and we got a taste for it, we cook it still, we like it that's why, we taste like it, Frankie, we're full completely full of it." Frankie shook her head like she'd given up, hands to her forehead run through her hair like she'd had it

"Maybe I don't give a fuck about the coming insurrection maybe I just give a fuck about you, Lily, about—" yeah? "I stayed for you Lil" she said. She shrugged. A big space where music might have started, not singing but music, some sound which filled the gap with something they could both understand because they could feel it. "You didn't need to stay to be an anarchist, you could be an anarchist anywhere" "I didn't stay to be a fucking anarchist I stayed to be a fucking dyke, Lily, to be by you so I could feel like a man like a boy for you, that's why I stayed I could be an anarchist anywhere of course I fucking could, fuck I could be a dyke anywhere, I could be a dyke anywhere I wanted, I stayed to be by you" "I know that" she said "I know I know" gah! Gaaah! "I can't stop imagining the future" this is anarchism (Frankie) talking of course "it's all I've ever thought of" pacing around the room packing packing "a new millennia. Is it hope?" stuffing clothes into bags push push "Frank stop" "Is it?" "Hope?" "Am I hopeful?" a fistful of t shirts and an open bag "Yes it's hope" "For who?" push, push "our children wouldn't be anarchists" Lily stands among it, not packing anything, not moving "there'd be no need to be" pack pack no not with "me as their father" pack pack I'd be anarchism enough "for them I'd never stop" stuffing t shirts into the bag "going on and on" soft stuffed bag like a teddy bear "for the kid? For who?" up, up "I can't stop, Lil,

134

this fine future, it's glowing in my mind I can't stop"
stuffing a suit jacket I can't stop "trying to find it to
get it started turning it over and over" Lily watching
what she's packing thinking yeah, yeah, you'll need
that that that, yeah, take that and that and it's just
layers of t shirts just the soft furnishings of Frankie's
body which Lily'd thought one day she'd take with
her someplace but they couldn't decide "the future"
Frankie's saying "it's never here" but they couldn't
decide where "The future was always here Frank" Lily
says exhausted "we spoke about it here and here and
here" she points at the sofa, at the bed, at the sink,
Frankie's fist tangled in ties "I'm fucking annoyed
at myself that's all" pushes them into the bag "not
at you at myself because now's done for, it's done
for, completely over." Pushes them into the bag not
at "you, Lil I'm not annoyed at you it's time, you
said it (Lily'd said: "It's just time") it's just now's the
right time. What if I become a broken heart and
that's it. An all-singing all-dancing broken heart like
an all-singing all-dancing hot dog or an all-singing
all-dancing peanut? What if I'm a heart that can sing
and dance and that's it? Not do what a heart is meant
to which I suppose is pump blood all around and love
that's the worry, really. Not even beat! HA!" Frankie
claps her hand too her forehead "not even a rhythm."
And Lily still thought Frankie was crushingly beautiful, iridescent like salmon, like candle sticks. And

Frankie still thought Lily slowed time whenever she appeared. That she made the air go thick and shiny around her like blown glass but they wouldn't see each other now. So Frankie wouldn't be opalescent, and Lily wouldn't smear time. Instead they would have to see what they were in other people's eyes. Maybe they would look rose-colored or maybe they'd seem solid and every time somebody saw them they'd imagine clambering onto their backs and looking out at things they'd never imagined anyone else could show them. But they didn't know that now. They had no sense of what they'd see in other people or of what other people would see in them.

Now! Sidney was planning something. [I'm planning something] Sid looked you in the eyes and said it [scuse me?] Suddenly Sid's just smoking a cigarette again [I thought you said something] [nah] Sid says. Not me. Sid was planning a big number, a big finale, a showstopper. Sid had been arrested once or twice for wearing slacks. You think that's the worst I can do? Sid said, you should see what I can stuff in them. Sid walks into the city bank like a scarecrow stiff with explosives her slacks stuffed with sticks of dynamite. The butch stands still at the center of the bank her slacks stuffed. The butch reaches into her breast pocket and pulls out a half-full soft pack of

Camels. She gives it a sharp flick of the wrist, and two cigarettes shoot out of the pack a half inch and a quarter inch respectively. Raising the pack slowly to her mouth, the butch takes the end of the longer cigarette between her lips and pulls it free. She tucks the pack back into her breast pocket, then pulls her zippo from her hip pocket. The butch is an anarchist and her slacks are stuffed with dynamite. She crooks her elbow, raising the lighter. Slowly, deliberately, she flicks open the lid so that it rings. Once or twice Sid had been arrested for wearing slacks. Just for slacks? You think that's the worst I can do? You should see what I can stuff in them. Sid walks into the prison stiff legged like a cowboy. Yes the police had really drawn Sid's attention to the slacks she'd never realized she was wearing really the focus they had put on them how much trouble slacks could cause had weaponized slacks in Sid Stein's mind. Sid walks into the prison, legs apart walking like a cowboy a bulge in her underwear the size of a bomb because it is. The butch spreads her legs, balancing her weight on the balls of her feet. She holds the comb ready to her hair, the fingers of her other hand extended, ready to smooth stray ends if necessary. She leans over to the side, bending away from the side she will be combing, tilting her head toward the comb. Her elbows jut until they are almost horizontal. She squints, concentrates, and then she lowers the comb. She will not comb

137

her hair just yet—there is something more she wishes to do to show off. Roz is in the deli when Sid comes in. Her slacks look packed. Roz watches as Sid walks stiffly over to the counter and orders a shake [SHAKE] and as she takes her first suck on the straw her slicked-back hair quivers. Time slows. The air goes thick [THICK] and slowly the sky realizes that Sid's slacks have exploded! The happy bomb! Milkshake across the pastrami sky. The sky grabs the deli and pulls it upwards coffee pooouurrrsss and Roz comes charging in: a shooting star with a winning smile winking in the sky. *Belle jjuuuuiiiiiiiiivvveeee* she roars grabbing hold of Sid's jacket slung over her shoulder just as Sid's body launches 5—her pack of cigarettes turn into a jet pack—4—and the two—3—are getting out of here—2—are getting out of here—1—they're a rocket ship leaving black smoke and grease in the sky *geeettfuuuccckkeedddd* Sid calls out and Roz remembers it's a Friday and shouts to her buddy "Where are the others?" and Sid says we'll see them all there and the week tears up in the atmosphere Sid's greasy engine sputters puck puck pucking its cigarette packet jet pack up with Roz the shimmering tail of the comet kaboom! Exploding Sid slouches through the sky she thinks she sees Frankie and calls out "I did it Frankie!" and Roz calls out "You've really done it now!"

[Once More with Feeling: It's Friday Night at the Bar!] "Time at the bar." That was the last thing Joanne said. It was a type of kindness, to remind them all before they stepped back out into it, that time had been happening this whole time. As much as they dug their heels in and gritted their teeth and even as much as they held onto one another, time was out there and it was in here too, now: time at the bar. "I'd rather set myself on fire" Marg said, putting down a jack and picking up a card the others couldn't see "What you scared of Margy?" "Zip it sparky I'm scared of blowing my body to bits up in space, you happy now?" They cackled "Yeah me too Marg I'm with you I'll wave you boys off but I'd rather wait it out here" "Right here in fact" "Yeah right here" Vic slapped down an ace and picked up something and Laur picked the ace straight up and put down another jack on top of Marg's "Well I'll send you a postcard" said Laur "*Greetings From Outta Space.*" The jukebox played Patsy Cline I Fall to Pieces. Teddy hummed along to it on key. He put down two more jacks and spread the four out in front of him and started again "You'd probably recognize those guys up there" they cackled "Oh hey Laur!" slapping their thighs waving like aliens would wave doing alien voices and Laur gives Vic a look across the table. I Will Follow Him by Peggy March comes on the jukebox. "I got nothing" says Marg and reaches down and sweeps the

cards up in her big hands and shuffles them leaving
the cigarette in her mouth. I love him I love him I
love him and where he goes I'll follow I'll follow I'll
follow. Vic stands up. She walks around the table,
bends her knees and keeps her back straight and
picks Laur up like a stagehand picks up a prop. She
hoists her over her shoulder and Laur hangs there
and doesn't struggle. And Vic walks them out of the
bar and keeps walking. "If the rest of my life was this
it'd be alright" Laur says, over Vic's shoulder "and I
could stop thinking about feeding myself and sleeping somewhere" "No more thinking kid" Vic says and
keeps walking all the way to Cains Warehouse where
the scenery was stored from all the folded Broadway
plays. They'd live there "We got everything we need
here" "Mmmm" "You wanna sofa to crash on we got a
hundred" mmm "you wanna stand under a lamppost
and lean and smoke and wait for a girl to come by?
Pick a post we've got streets of them" mmm "you
wanna play cowboys? Play rich people? Play army?
Play house?" mmmm "It's all here." Vic propped Laur
up against a bar, "Last call" she said.

THE ANNUAL MEETING
OF THE BOP

Friends, Comrades, Piano Players, Distinguished
Guests, thank you for coming to the annual meeting
of the BOP. This year we've been working hard to
entertain you [cheer] to be the players instead of the
people getting played [laughter]. We thank the bar
owners for listening to our demands and we thank the
bargoers for listening to our music. And I thank my
comrades. I know pianists aren't usually a part of the
marching band, but here at the BOP we're here to tell
you we'll march if we have to [cheer and voice louder
over cheers keeping on] we'll stamp our feet if we have
to [louder!] we'll stop sitting on our stools and stand
up! [cheer] stand up! [and the pianists in the audience
stand up and the audience follows standing up and
raising their glasses] and I know, I know, that usually
there's only one piano player in the band [it quietens
down, they're listening nodding their heads slowly]
and so I thank my comrades for showing me just what
a whole band of piano players can do. [Cheers, cheers!

some tears in some eyes including the speakers] So, let's hear it, raise your glasses, to the Butch On Piano [*to the butch on piano*] and they drink.

Lily wasn't a very good drinker, it made her bendy and she slurred and slurring didn't mean anything to Lily. Lily was sharp or she was quiet. Frankie'd liked that. Frankie was a singer and she did. "Yeah when we were kids we pushed each other down hills in the park" "Oh so you really go back a while" "Yeah back to rolling down hills age" "Way back then" "Oh way back." Lily'd spotted her. "Frankie?" Frankie turned round to look, like a person would turn to look if they could manage it after having had a knife plunged between their shoulder blades. Lily had known they'd all be there. Sammy Silver'd said: "We'll all be there, at the annual meeting, all the union members and we're playing you know? So Frankie, Frankie'll be there too" "I'm invited aren't I?" Lily said and Sammy Silver'd sighed. Lily could have fallen in love with Sammy, this first one, and Sammy would have sat her on top of her piano and wheeled her round the city and when she'd have been tired Sammy would have opened the lid of the piano and she'd have crawled inside it and yawned and Sammy would have touched her lips with her piano fingers and she'd have slept under the lid on the strings, pushing the keys when she breathed. But it had been Frankie. Frankie turns around: "Lily" There she was, Frankie: one long curl between her eyes, the sleeves of her shirt pushed up over her elbows and her top pocket spilling all sorts of things. Looking at Lily the way she always had, like she was the severed head of a king and on the stage the host said "Our first act of the evening, a pillar of the BOP and comrade to piano players everywhere, ladies and gentlemen, your Harry Harlem." But the spotlight, as the light dimmed, seemed to land on Lily and Frankie, reunited. And you can hear Frankie's heart beating and see Lily sway. And Frankie reaches out and then back. And Lily reaches for her then stops. And Frankie turns her head away again and turns it back [and Harry's playing] and Lily holds her head steady and tries to keep it together and Frankie's heart beats da dum da dum da dum da—and Lily's heart whirrs and Frankie shuffles her feet [and Harry's playing] and the sound of their breathing is like a wind section—dum mmm ah da dum mmm ah da dum—and their hearts are beating da dum da dum da dum da—their arms are reaching out and back and out and back like a string section da dum mmm ah zzzz da dum mmm ah zzzz da dum mmm ah zzzz and though Harry's playing they can't hear it over all the music they're made of together, over all the memories of how they played. "Fancy a dance Lil?" It's Sammy, upstanding member of the

BOP and Lily's date. Harry's music floods in now. "Hey, you must be Frankie, good to meet you, you and Lily are old friends so she's told me, and Sammy Silver said, said you all were Red Diapers" "Goldman Babies" Frankie says loudly over Harry's music which fills the room and makes each guest feel as if they are a black key or a white key being pressed gently on their heads and dipped under Harry's touch and their bodies vibrate, go from cold ivory to warm music, touch, touch, touch "Of course of course" Sammy says, and Frankie says "Yeah when we were kids we pushed each other down hills in the park" "Oh so you really go back a while" "Yeah back to rolling down hills age" "Way back then" "Oh way back."

"The best part" Frankie Gold and Sammy Silver are together at a table, "is playing." The party goes on around them. They've always been gentle together. Everything about Frankie's life and Sammy's life had been gentle even when it was hard even when it was violent even when it was to do with dying or with really going for it really playing [plonk plonk plonk on the piano and singing until your lungs hurt] gently it had come upon a rising tide the way anarchism comes like a spring. Someone left the tap on, Sammy said, and now here we are. She stressed the we:

"Someone left the tap on" [Sammy] "and now here we are" as if they were clouds. And to what portent? "What'll it be?" Sammy asked "What is ours?" Frankie asked "Howsit feel?" Sammy asked "What's it sound like?" "Can you hear it?" "Are you hungry?" "Is it over?" "Do we have to?" They asked questions and never answered them knowing answers don't rise. The scene is them sitting together in the carpeted hall at the annual meeting of the BOP. The mood is carpeted and red and around them people move and meet and sway and somebody's singing and cheering and some people dance. At the table beside them Louis says to somebody "Swing's over" "Bebop's done" and the blues stays like a siren. At the table next to them Frankie and Sammy finish each other's sentences "We never went "back and forth "nothings ever "ended it's always "just "just been going on "I know "what "you're about to tell me how you love "the moment we take a bow" "I knew it!" Sammy said shaking her head. "You're a broken record Frankie" "You're a gold tooth Sam" "You're a butter knife Frankie, that's what you are" "You're silver Sam" "You're gold" wet stones and lap lap "I do love it though!" "Tell me again" Sammy wanted to hear it "I love taking a bow Sam, how at the end once we've played, you and I, I turn around" "You turn around" "And you're there" "And there I am" "And you stand up and I turn back to the crowds" "They're all there" "And I know it's done" "For tonight" "And we take a bow."

"I have been your host this evening!" Frankie imagines what it would be like to stop the music, whether the show would sound so different? Sammy would be kind of miming the piano. Or the piano would become a typewriter and as Frankie spoke as if she were about to sing she would be accompanied, as she always was, by Sammy clack clacking on the typewriter keys. Sammy would touch the keys on the score a, a, a, e, e, bbb cccc dd eee ff ggg spools and spools of paper with only octaves on, a b c d e f g she'd type it, over and over whenever the music told her to and in front of her she'd see Frankie, the back of her, the part of her she saw the most. The wiggly line where her hair wiggled down her neck her collar getting wet in the stage lights and the packet of cigarettes in her back pocket so she could reach for them almost as soon as she'd got off the stage "You wanna sing again?" Sammy'd say and snuff it out and Frankie'd say "After that performance?" Sammy wanted to walk across the stage and hold Frankie round the waist and call her comrade. Sammy wondered if Frankie sometimes forgot she was behind her. If she was only company, a buffer against complete aloneness. But Frankie could feel Sammy behind her like a spine.

To Frankie Sammy accompanied her the way bones accompany muscle. Frankie would bend backwards completely, would wiggle and wave without Sammy behind her. "Comrade!" Sammy'd call and Frankie'd turn and she'd grab hold of her, hold her arms down tightly to her sides as if she'd come to collect her, to take her away, she'd squeeze and squeeze her, Sammy's strong arms around Frankie softly lit in the stage lights but Sammy had never done it and she needn't have because Frankie'd felt as if she were being held by Sammy the whole time. The way the most accomplished accompanist holds their players. They'd played together. Sometimes they had played such fine *fine* music. Had had nights where the audi ence had melted away for both of them, and they both knew, they both knew without telling each other or sometimes Frankie'd turn and wink at her *this is it* she'd wink *the whole world's here now* the stage had become something else more like a country of their own, and suddenly they knew at once together with- out having to say it that they wished the stage would be rushed. That the audience, the bartenders, the doormen and the people outside would rush in, rush and rush up onto the stage to this new country they'd made. Sometimes they played like that. Oh they'd played together. They had played. "But did they hear us?" Frankie asked "not what I was singing but what I meant by it? Did they hear it Sam? Do they know or should I have said it?" Now Frankie Gold and Sammy Silver take the stage at the annual meeting of the BOP where all the factions of the butch piano players union have been mingling this evening, have been making eyes and shaking hands and creating little rumbles when they tap their feet. Frankie looks out across the hall, Sammy behind her at the piano. In the audience Lily closes her eyes, not against it, but so as to be more there, there more. She closes her eyes and sees Frankie singing and Sammy on piano. Just the three of them, apart from next to her with her eyes open the other Sammy, the one she loved now, maybe, or certainly loved the feel of, how her lips felt and her hands felt and the look of her certainly loved the look of her, her jawline and her fingernails. And certainly the sound of her, she loved the sound of her how her rings clacked on the piano when you sat near to her as she played and she reached for sharps yes the sound her pinky ring made, a tiny clack against the edge of the black keys. Yes she loved that. But still she closed her eyes now and it was just the three of them, how they'd played. And Frankie saw Lily in the audience with her eyes closed and imagined she was playing in the living room some Friday night in the past and the audience were crowded on the carpet of Asha's apartment "Comrades" she said "I know you've heard of syncopation, but how about syndication? This is the era of hard bop" sounds as though she's about to sing but Frankie's thinking maybe she won't this time. Behind her, Sammy Silver's piano turns into a typewriter clack clack clack like someone had put a microphone to the tiny tapping of Sammy's pinky ring and somehow it still sounds like music. "The best orators" Asha used to say "sound as though at any moment they are about to sing that they might burst into song, that they might burst" that's the feeling of it, Frankie'd thought and she'd said it "Comrades I know you've felt as I do, as though you might burst" the butches shuffle "I always say, I shoulda been a talker not a singer" "You are!" "Alright alright!" Frankie smiles and looks like a boy and Lily closes her eyes and sees them, the three of them in a room all the middle parts cut out, and Frankie sings right to her or is she speaking? "Remember nights at Rosa's?" "Who me?" "Of course you Lil, who else is listening?" the butches shuffle "I remember nights" "Just the three of us" like a chord "Oh I don't remember it ever being just the three of us" Sammy says "Life was always busier than that" "You're right" "It was always the three of us" "And everybody else" "Of course" "Isn't that it?" "Yeah that's it, Frank" Frankie'd never worn a coat that wasn't everybody's. "Wouldn't it be a *grand* piano?" Frankie said now to the whole room eyes wide, no spotlights just everybody at the BOP lit up, all the members and all their guests [shuffle] "a *grand* piano which stretched to octaves so low they'd

always catch us. And stretched so high, so high—"
surely *now* she'd sing "so high we'd never reach it
just dream of it such a long, long piano that all of
us could sit down at and play. A *grand* piano, isn't
that the truth?" Shouts from the crowd: "And you
could take a seat wherever you liked at it?" "Sure
you could!" "And you could play whatever notes you
wanted?" "Of course you could!" "And you could eat
your dinner off it!" "Always" "And you could crawl
up under it" "For shelter" "For shelter" "And all the
notes we all played, all the melodies they'd sound
so sweet together" cheer cheer! "they'd sound like
a music we could never compose on our own our
little lonely melodies those strains I've been singing
all these nights on all the stages all these shows I'm
wondering what it'd sound like if we all sang, you
understand, if we all played" cheer cheer "it wouldn't
sound like music at all" "It'd sound like overflowing!"
"Yes Yes Yes!" "But maybe *overflowing*" Frankie said
"is a perfectly fine type of over."

NOTES

All quotations included/adapted in the novel are cited here and quoted in their original form.

p. 24 "(Closing time was 4 a.m., when everybody went around to Reuben's, the people who invented the sandwich, on East 58th Street, just off Fifth, with the after-hours crowd, or up to Harlem.)"

—Lisa E. Davis. "The Butch as Drag Artiste: Greenwich Village in the Roaring Forties" in *The Persistent Desire; a Femme–Butch Reader,* edited by Joan Nestle. Alyson Publications, 1992.

p. 26 "Now Tevye might condone modern love, […] he might even shrug his shoulders at revolution with its crazy "what's yours is mine, what's mine is yours" but he will never condone apostasy […] For the essence of Tevye is his religion, it is his chief raison d'etre, the condition of his survival; and if he condoned his daughter's apostasy, he would become something very much less than Tevye…"

—Frances Butwin. "Introduction" to *Tevye's Daughters* by Sholom Aleichem, translated by Frances Butwin. Vallentine, Mitchell & Co., 1973.

p. 33 "She lives in the hope that very soon the pot will boil over, as they say, the sun will rise and everything become bright. He will be set free along with many others like him, and then, she says, they will all roll up their sleeves and get to work to turn the world upside down.

—Sholom Aleichem. "Chava" in *Tevye's Daughters*, translated by Frances Butwin. Vallentine, Mitchell & Co., 1973.

p. 104 "A shape with lion body and the head of a man,
A gaze blank and pitiless as the sun,
Is moving its slow thighs, while all about it
Reel shadows of the indignant desert birds.
The darkness drops again; but now I know
That twenty centuries of stony sleep
Were vexed to nightmare by a rocking cradle,
And what rough beast, its hour come round
          at last,
Slouches towards Bethlehem to be born?

—W.B. Yeats. "The Second Coming"

p. 136 "Now the butch reaches into her breast pocket and
-137 pulls out a half-full soft pack of Camels. She gives it a sharp flick of the wrist, and two cigarettes shoot out of the pack a half inch and a quarter inch respectively. Raising the pack slowly to her mouth, the butch takes the end of the longer cigarette between her lips and pulls it free. She tucks the pack back into her breast pocket, then pulls

her zippo from her hip pocket. She crooks her elbow, raising the lighter. Slowly, deliberately, she flicks open the lid so that it rings," and "The butch spreads her legs, balancing her weight on the balls of her feet. She holds the comb ready to her hair, the fingers of her other hand extended, ready to smooth stray ends if necessary. She leans over to the side, bending away from the side she will be combing, tilting her head toward the comb. Her elbows jut until they are almost horizontal. She squints, concentrates, and then she lowers the comb. She will not comb her hair just yet—there is something more she wishes to do to show off."

—Merril Mushroom. "How the Butch Does it: 1959" in *The Persistent Desire; a Femme-Butch Reader*, edited by Joan Nestle. Alyson Publications, 1992.

ACKNOWLEDGMENTS

Deep gratitude to Nightboat. The joyous full margins of chat with Lindsey+Trisha+Lina+Gia=this now! For those years of guidance, thanks to Peter and Isabel. THANK YOU DEVA!!!

NIGHTBOAT BOOKS

Nightboat Books, a nonprofit organization, seeks to develop audiences for writers whose work resists convention and transcends boundaries. We publish books rich with poignancy, intelligence, and risk. Please visit nightboat.org to learn about our titles and how you can support our future publications.

The following individuals have supported the publication of this book. We thank them for their generosity and commitment to the mission of Nightboat Books:

Kazim Ali • Anonymous (8) • Mary Armantrout • Jean C. Ballantyne • Thomas Ballantyne • Bill Bruns • John Capetta • V. Shannon Clyne • Ulla Dydo Charitable Fund • Photios Giovanis • Amanda Greenberger • Vandana Khanna • Isaac Klausner • Shari Leinwand • Anne Marie Macari • Elizabeth Madans • Martha Melvoin • Caren Motika • Elizabeth Motika • The Leslie Scalapino - O Books Fund • Robin Shanus • Thomas Shardlow • Rebecca Shea • Ira Silverberg • Benjamin Taylor • David Wall • Jerrie Whitfield & Richard Motika • Arden Wohl • Issam Zineh

This book is made possible, in part, by grants from the New York City Department of Cultural Affairs in partnership with the City Council, the New York State Council on the Arts Literature Program, and the National Endowment for the Arts.